Below the Surface

Arthur Hallam Elton

Contents

BELOW THE SURFACE

BY

Arthur Hallam Elton

BELOW THE SURFACE.

CHAPTER I

THE MANOR-HOUSE FARM.

THE Manor Farm was situated in a broad spacious valley winding between two lofty ranges of hill which ran nearly due east and west. As the eye followed their undulating sweep, and the abruptness with which they seemed to slope suddenly upwards from the level plain below, you could easily believe the popular tradition, that a wide and noble river, or even an arm of the sea, had once upon a time ebbed and flowed along that valley, now rich with green pastures and waving corn, and stately rows of elms; and had washed the base of those hills, jutting out into rocky promontories, sparely interspersed with ancient oaks, or receding into sheltered ravines, where larch and birch mixed their tender green with the foliage of the Scotch fir, almost black by contrast-Broad downs of close sweet herbage, on which sheep were feeding, rose above the woods and plantations which clothed the sides of these hills; and, as you followed the varying outlines of either side of the valley, now receding now advancing, you perceived the furthest vista shrouded miles away in a kind of purple haze, where the eye lost itself in uncertain conjecture.

A road which seemed tolerably frequented, wound along the valley, following pretty closely the outer edge of the first slope of hills on the southern side. It was occasionally lined by trim gardens, orchards whose thick-blossomed foliage, seen afar off, looked a cloud of delicate white smoke hanging stationary upon the green plains, and thatched cottages buried in roses and jessamine. Lower down in the valley, the grass and growing crops wore a ranker and more luxuriant aspect;

whilst occasional alder beds, and clumps of poplar, bore witness to the more humid character of the soil.

Now, out of this main road, at the entrance of a broad but not deeply-indented ravine, there ran a lane which ascended the hill northwards, and was soon lost in over-hanging trees of large growth.

Down one side of this lane flowed a brawling little transparent stream; but on the other was an ancient boundary wall, which might have enclosed a garden or park of some country-house or family mansion On descending the lane into the valley, this wall, as you joined the road below, ended in a large grove of trees; and, if you turned to the right along the main road, you would find beyond this grove, a spacious piece of pasture studded with clumps of trees, which sloped upwards for awhile towards the crest of the hill, but was soon lost in coppice and plantations.

This wide field was intersected by an avenue of noble elms, which commenced, indeed, half a mile off, in the marshy lands on the other side of the road; and, re-commencing again on the side we are describing, continued to cross the field until it blended with scattered elms at the foot of the hill. Apparently this had once led to some important mansion, situate in a park which had been since intersected by the main road. No such mansion was now, however, to be seen, although the avenue was one which many a man of wealth would have gladly given thousands to transplant bodily to his new-made park, fringed with juvenile plantations, and timid little pine-trees, fresh from the nearest nursery gardens, shivering inside their palisaded fences. There was no mansion, then, at the extreme end of this av-enue. A narrow carriage drive entered the field between the rows of elms, but soon branched off, inclining away in another direction until it conducted you to a fence of iron hurdles, which protected from intruding cattle a tolerably well-kept lawn and garden, where stood, close under the hill, with a background of elms, a long, low, old-fashioned, but not ancient, domicile, with latticed windows glittering in the sun, and a honeysuckled porch. It was a good-sized house enough, but evidently of more modern date than the grand old avenue which stretched across the park-like grounds in an oblique direction. If you went round the back of this house, and crossed a well-stocked kitchen garden, you would come to a scene which, by contrast, was to the tranquil and beautiful landscape we have been just regarding, one of excitement and bustle. For here you found, first, the roofs of huge barns partially visible, the gable ends of various buildings, the tawny thatch of wheat-mows and hay-stacks; then as you looked through a gateway, whose massive quoins denoted an earlier date than the house itself, leading into the stack-yards, you heard the loud lowing of oxen, the indignant grunting of pigs, the clamour of ducks and poultry, the occasional shouts of men, and the deep humming and throbbing of a steam-engine, thrashing corn.

To return, however, to the front of the house. Walking up and down the lawn in a quiet reflective manner, might be seen a man, clad plainly enough in a shooting-coat, trousers of coarse material, and low-crowned hat. He was young, rather tall then otherwise, and apparently of well-knit and active frame. Hitherto the reader might suppose him to be simply a tenant-farmer, renting land, and cultivating it in order to gain a living. On regarding him more narrowly, you saw, however, that there was something superior in his manner and bearing. He carried himself well; his head was erect; there was a general ease and self-possession in his gestures. Moreover, as he turned and you saw his face, you immediately recognised the thoughtful expression of one whose intellect has not merely been trained, but duly used and ex-ercised. His features were somewhat strongly marked; the nose aquiline, the chin, if anything, slightly prominent; but there was a calm, almost sad expression in his dark grey eyes, and a delicacy about the curve of his lip, which softened the severity of his countenance, and implied that his disposition, though possibly inclined to be methodical and exacting, was nevertheless affectionate and trustful.

Sometimes he stopped in his walk, and watched the sun shining over the western extremity of the valley, and descending slowly amidst long thin bars of glittering cloud, as down a gorgeous ladder. Sometimes he turned his head in the direction of the farmstead, and listened with apparent pleasure to the hum of the steam-engine mingling with the distant music of a blacksmith's forge; whilst, in the wood close at hand, a thrush poured forth its torrent of joyful, fearless, reckless melody. Then he marked the white smoke of the engine rising above the tree-tops behind the house, and streaming away until it was lost in the purple hills beyond; and, as he did so, he suddenly put his hand to his brow and resumed his walk at a quicker pace.

" Yes," he said to himself; " our life fades away like a vapour—like that wreath of smoke which is wafted over the hills'; and yet I muse and fret over the petty trials of the world, as if I were for ever tied to this plot ot ground, and had no other position to look forward to—no other inheritance to labour for but that I now see round me."

He took a few more turns, then added— "These people, these new-comers, the Usherwoods, shrink from me; strive to keep me at a distance; almost insult me by their frigid condescension. They seem to fear my intentions might become too pressing. As if I was not the last man to force myself into society where I am not welcome! Lady Maud regards me with an eye of pity, and repulses me as if it tore her heart to do so. The young ladies are mute in my pres-ence. Gertrude is as cold as marble." He paused: "Why do I call her Gertrude? I scarcely know her, yet my whole spirit leaped up when we first met, as if there was some secret link between us. How foolish a man is," he continued, in a more matter-of-fact tone—"when his heart is a little smitten! I believe, if it had not been for Miss Usher-wood, I should never have gone near the house after first calling there. But she, Miss Usherwood— it's so long, the name, I must call her Gertrude—Gertrude so took my fency, that I have actually called twice. It's not love; no, nothing of the kind; it's a foolish, abstract sort of admiration for what is beautiful. I must guard against it, I must in-deed." And he crumpled up a rosebud he had just plucked, with an expression as if he had settled that matter at once, and for ever. " I shall not go near the house again, unless invited."

At that moment the loud baying of dogs from the adjacent stables and farm-yard rising above the milder uproar usual in those quarters, shewed that strangers were approaching the premises.

The rumble of wheels next reached the ear, and presently a fashionable landau was seen rolling along the carriage drive, until it came to a full stop at the low iron gate leading into the lawn. A powdered footman blazing with lace, sprang down, and gracefully tripped to open the gate, but was anticipated by our friend, who held it open whilst the coachman drove through at a foot's pace, and pulled up in front of the house, looking seriously mortified at being compelled, by the contracted size of the lawn, to bring up his cattle at a funeral walk instead of an animated trot.

Within the carriage reclined an elderly gentleman and a lady apparently his wife, who had still a very good share of freshness and bloom in her countenance. She had once evidently been a very pretty creature, and though now rather large and matronly, presented, of an evening especially, a decidedly winning appearance. She was fair, with clear-cut, regular features; a dimpled chin; hair of a rich brown, which once had reached her waist, and even now retained a respectable degree of luxuriance. The principal charm of her face, however, was her eyes of soft blue, generally dreamy, absent, and vague in their expression, but ever and anon lighting up with a brilliancy which seemed to pierce you, gently but irresistibly, through and through. Her companion was a less interesting individual. A stout old gentleman, with swarthy complexion, dark bushy eyebrows, and an eye not unintelligent, but of that character which im-plies an inability to take in more than one idea at a time. There was something now and then humorous in the expression of his countenance, as if he did not object to a joke; but he never laughed without glancing at his lady as if to ask permission. Not that he was what is called "henpecked;" Lady Maud Usherwood would never have condescended to any such vulgar method of having her own way. He was in a state of willing subserviency to her, and it was his joy and pride so to be. We may just add that he wore an unexceptional costume, for it was entirely superintended by Lady Maud. The only blemish was an enormous watch chain, which proclaimed to the civilized world that he carried a watch. This he had asked leave to wear with almost tears in his eyes; for it had belonged to his grandfather, and this concession Lady Maud, with her usual tact, had promptly accorded to him.

" Mr. Nugent!" exclaimed Lady Maud, leaning gracefully out of the carriage window—"Mr. Nugent, I am shocked you should have had this trouble. Our men are so slow in opening gates after a season in town"

" Mr. Nugent!" echoed Mr. Usherwood, "I am shocked that the clumsiness of our servants, recently returned from the metropolis, should have occasioned you this trouble;" and so, saying, Mr. Usherwood bowed until his head vanished beneath the side of the carriage

Nugent, raising his hat from his head with grave politeness, assisted his visitors to descend. He was a good deal perplexed by the unexpected honour paid him, and still more by the alteration of tone and manner perceptible in both his visitors, but particularly in Mr. Usherwood.

Lady Maud was rarely severe or crushing. She froze you like a moonbeam, or blew you delicately away like a feather. Like that eastern potentate who, commiserating the fears of a criminal about to be put to death, drew a gleaming, almost impalpable, scimitar round his neck, and then soothingly requested him to shake the head, which at the instant, fell severed to the ground; so Lady Maud annihilated her victim with an equally merciful dexterity, and it was with almost tears of gratitude that he succumbed to her tender but inevitable stroke.

Nugent, therefore, welcomed them with politeness, but with some degree of coldness and hauteur. He led them into the house, and shewed them into an apartment dimly lighted, which, in his bachelor condition, Kas only used on state occasions. The furniture was tolerably handsome, but the curtains and cushions of sombre hue, and every thing bore that aspect of excruciating neatness which characterises a rarely-frequented room. Chairs ranged with scrupulous regularity round the table, upon which thirteen books were placed at equal distances from each other, as if thirteen individuals were hourly expected to arrive, and devote themselves to their perusal. A housemaid, almost in a state of temporary insanity, had just before rushed into the room, hearing the noise of approaching carriage-wheels, and opened the shutters and windows; but the atmosphere was still close and damp, in fact, we may say sepulchral. There was nothing in the books or ornaments of the room to denote that the owner was devoted to agricultural pursuits. The books were, many of them, on religious subjects: there were very few pictures except family portraits, done in chalk, and mildewed to a degree which distressingly impaired the beauty of the individuals portrayed, if beauty they ever indeed possessed; there were no flowers; there was no piano.

Lady Maud, who always ascertained at a glance the bright side of things (where there was any bright side at all), glided to the window, and began to praise the prettiness of the view. Mr. Usherwood stepped to another window, and also praised the view, omitting to notice, until he came close, that the Venetian blind was drawn down. Nevertheless, it was a pretty view. A slope of well-kept lawn rising upwards from the house, and ending in a mass of evergreens overshadowed by fir-trees, and a few large.elms and walnut-trees. There were some formal flower-beds on the lawn; they were only furnished with a confused mass of common perennial flowers, but looked blooming and pleasant. On the right, the kitchen-garden wall shut out all view of the farm-buildings, and against the outside of this wall trailed an abundant growth of flowering creepers, with now and then a well-trained apricot or fig-tree.

" Would your ladyship like to step out, and give the garden a nearer inspection ? " asked Nugent.

" Of all things !" was the rejoinder, and throwing open the window, which reached to the ground, they all issued forth.

" This is a sweet spot!" cried Lady Maud, gently, almost timidly, taking Nugent's arm.

"A veryagreeable tenement,"added the old gentleman.

" Why," said Nugent, who was a little, and but a little mollified by the soft looks and words of his fair companion—" It is perhaps too pretty for a mere man of business, such as I am. It was always kept up in old times, and I don't like to let it run to waste, or to grub it up."

"You term yourself a man of business," remonstrated Lady Maud, " as if you bent over a desk or counter all day. Now, I consider agriculture to be one part business, and three parts pleasure."

"A happy mixture of work and play"—put in Mr. Usherwood.

"Ah!" replied Nugent, "it's a serious enough matter for me. I am a regular farmer, and I am proud of the name and the occupation."

"That's right!" cried Mr. Usherwood; "speed the plough, say I." And the worthy gentleman, in his sudden access of enthusiasm, was about to pat Nugent encouragingly on the back; but, noticing the expression of his countenance, thought better of it, and, taking out his handkerchief, elaborately blew his nose.

" O, you know, Mr. Nugent," observed Lady Maud, " that our object in calling here to-day, was partly to ask you to show us all over your beautiful farm-buildings, and let us see your cattle and machines, and the wonderful things you use in what you modestly designate your ' business.' "

Nugent's countenance slightly brightened as he expressed his readiness to comply with her request, "But," he added, "if you intend to explore all my workshop thoroughly, you need have some better defence for your feet than those thin boots, Lady Maud. And as for you, sir, you will find pumps rather worse than nothing."

"Oh! we are provided with goloshes — both Mr. Usherwood and myself,—if you will kindly send to the carriage, they are wrapped up in a parcel in the pockets."

After a few minutes spent in these preparations, the party sallied forth.

They crossed the kitchen-garden and the narrow drive which separated it from the farm-stead, then entered the stack-yard through the ancient archway we have already mentioned; whence by a private door they passed into another large yard, three sides of which were composed of various buildings in good condition and of massive construction, most of them like the archway of seemingly very ancient date, or else built with the materials of some building belonging to the past. One long shed contained forty or fifty steers and heifers, in a state of lively enjoyment, ranged side by side, and consuming steamed hay and chaff, mixed with Swede turnips reduced to pulp by a crushing machine. At the moment the party entered this yard, a door at the opposite side was suddenly opened, and out rushed, gamboling, stumbling, jostling together, a score or so of young calves recently weaned. Now, to the unpractised eye of Mr. Usherwood, this apparition seemed nothing else than a vast herd of infuriated oxen, or viciously-disposed cows. He hastily retreated to the archway whence he had just emerged, whilst even Lady Maud, either from alarm, or the impulse of newly-awakened friendship, pressed her arm for a moment closer to Nugent's side.

"I give my young stock," explained Nugent, unconscious of the alarm pervading one at least of his companions, " a good game of play here twice a-day. They need, like all of us, a little recreation."

" The pretty creatures!" cried Lady Maud; " I wish they would come nearer."

Nugent stepped forward upon the heap of fresh straw which thickly coated the centre of the yard, and the calves thronged round him impatiently, as if to communicate some information of importance.

" Mind your glove, ma'am!" shouted one of Nugent's men, accompanying the caution by a thump with the handle of a pick on the back of an enterprising calf, which, stimulated by Lady Maud's playful attempt to stroke its forehead, had begun to beslobber her delicately-gloved hand with its wet, nutmeg-grater tongue.

" Oh, I enjoy it! "—exclaimed Lady Maud; "don't hurt the dear creature. I adore calves!"

Mr. Usherwood, whose intimacy with calves had been maintained exclusively through the medium of veal-pie and calves' foot jelly, thought it expedient now to emerge from the archway, and also profess an almost idolatrous fondness for those animals. Nugent, however, now led them onwards to another yard, where the black steam-engine was emitting a steady volume of smoke from its chimney. A rustic stoker, who superintended it, appeared to view its performances with pride and satisfaction, and remarked to Nugent—

" He's terrible hungry, and swallows a sight of coal!" whilst a grin of satisfaction .diffused itself over his blackened face. Behind the engine, the threshing-machine was clamorously at work, connected by a leather strap with the motive power of the steam engine. Men and women, half hid in a cloud of dust, which caused Mr. Usherwood to sneeze, as Lady Maud afterwards assured him—" like a demon "—were busy in supplying the wheat sheaves to be threshed, and otherwise regulating and superintending the work.

Elsewhere, under an open shed, some men were engaged dissolving bones in sulphuric acid, and mixing ashes with guano. Here Mr. Usherwood, sniffing the air, remarked that he liked the smell of guano, it was associated with luxuriant crops. Lady Maud made no remark, but possibly was comparing the ammonia of the manure with the ammonia of the bottle of Preston salts she was pensively pressing to her nose. They passed on, and came upon women and lads bearing pails of frothy milk, fresh from the cows, in the milking barton. From an adjacent building, oozed a savoury smoke from the fodder and victuals, steaming in preparation for cattle, horses, and pigs. Two teams of splendid horses, and the same number of oxen, crossed slowly into an adjoining yard; the latter encouraged by not unmelodious cries from the boy who drove them. A dozen or more score of South-down sheep were slowly ascending the slope of a neighbouring eminence on their way to a piece of arable, where they were to be folded during the night. These required, from time to time, rather pressing intimations from a couple of sheep-dogs to keep moving.

The scene was animated, and not without its peculiar charm. Every one was busy; order and promptitude reigned throughout; the very clamours which filled the air possessed a certain affinity one with another; and, spreading freely and widely in that pure and unconfined atmosphere, were not jarring to the ear, but blended into a kind of rude harmony.

Lady Maud was just asking Nugent how he could bring himself to sell the beautiful dove-coloured oxen, pointed out to her in one of the sheds, for vulgar butcher s meat, when a dismal groan from Mr. Usher-wood burst upon their ears from an adjoining yard, and that poor gentleman was speedily discovered, standing up to his ankles in mud, amidst a multitude of pigs of all sorts and sizes. He feared to move lest he should sink deeper into the treacherous mire, yet was sorely embarrassed by his swinish companions, who, having at first retreated from their unknown visiter, were now becoming unpleasantly familiar, thrusting their long snouts between his legs at the imminent risk of upsetting him, rubbing against his knees with grunts of satisfaction, and, in short, exhibiting a hospitable and friendly feeling, which he by no means seemed to appreciate.

" I can't move an inch!" shouted the old gentleman; " I shall be up to my neck the moment I put one foot forward! Bring a ladder, or a rope, or something !"

Nugent rushed to the rescue, and succeeded, knowing the geographical ins and outs of the mud, in steering Mr. Usherwood back to *terra firma*, with the loss only of a golosh, which was doubtless regarded by the pigs as a parting tribute of regard. The party now returned to the garden, and from thence re-entered the house.

In the entrance passage, however, stood a man respect-ably dressed, looking rather like an upper servant out of place. He was pale and careworn, and his light-grey eyes seemed restless and suspicious, but he was other-wise not ill-looking.

"Well, Weston," asked Nugent, "and how's your sister?"

"Much the same, sir, thank you. I am come to trouble you again for a little drop of wine. It is such horrid stuff they sell at the ' Red Lion.' Money won't get the sort of wine Lucy requires."

" Go and sit down, and you shall have some in a few minutes."

" 'Tis Lucy Weston, Lady Maud," he added, turning to her ladyship. " One of your ladyship's servants who has been so ill lately."

" Oh, Lucy!" rejoined Lady Maud, slightly blushing. " Yes, poor thing! I wonder my people have not sent her what she wants. Will she recover ? "

" I intend to see her to-morrow at twelve, and will let your ladyship know how she is."

" Will you not be in some danger ? I heard it was a horrid kind of fever," asked Lady Maud.

"I am not afraid of infection, with proper precautions," rejoined Nugent; and his visiters after warm expressions of admiration for all they had seen, prepared to take their departure. Lady Maud pressed his hand gently. Mr. Usherwood gave it a confidential gripe.

They got into their carriage, assisted by Nugent with considerably more em-presaement than he had evinced in helping them out, and, when whirled out of sight, were still gesticulating a polite farewell from either window.

Nugent watched them for a while, then walked slowly back to the house with an expression of perplexity very plainly visible on his countenance.

CHAPTER II

PLANS AND PROSPECTS.

" WELL, my love!" exclaimed Mr. Usherwood, as the carriage, having gained the main road, rolled briskly away towards home; " as we have gone through this precious ceremony (and I am sure, for my part, I deserve great credit for my performance), perhaps you will condescend to inform me why you have taken such a sudden fancy to this Nugent; this mighty farmer, whose great-grandfather, legend says, was a gentleman? "

"My dear," replied the lady, "you are severe. His father, grandfather, great-grandfather, were all gentlemen—thoroughbred, I assure you; and he is a gentleman—"

"He a gentleman?" inquired her husband incredulously, for his notion of the meaning of the word was not very precise. " He a gentleman ? "

" He is, my dear. He not only is, but, what is quite as much to the purpose, he looks a gentleman. His ancestors lived here centuries ago. There stood a great house there once upon a time. The very estate we have lately purchased belonged to him. The Nugents of Fitznugent are nearly connected with him. The Clintons of Llanellesmere are his cousins. A Herbert Nugent was hanged, drawn, and quartered by Henry VIII., for treason or heresy, I forget which. Lady Amelia Rosamunda de Clare (lately married to the eldest son of Sir Sampson Frogmorton), has certainly Nugent blood in her veins; and she, you know, is descended in a direct line from Sir James Tyrrell, who murdered the princes in the Tower."

Mr. Usherwood, quite overpowered by this array of facts, which Lady Maud uttered with graceful volubility, fell back in the carriage, and gazed admiringly at his wife. "But why," he, after a pause, inquired; "why this sudden affection for him ? A few days ago, we were all to turn the cold shoulder on him. Now, we are hail fellow and well met. Look at this shoe," he added, raising his foot carefully, " spoilt by the mud of your friend's farm-yard. And the pigs are at this moment mumbling my golosh!"

"My dear," said Lady Maud, "you have always had confidence in me, and I trust that confidence has not been misplaced."

" Maud," interrupted Mr, U., with responsive warmth, " your opinion is law with me: downright law."

" The fact is," continued Lady Maud, slightly lowering her voice, " I have received private information respecting Mr. Nugent's prospects, which has caused me much thought, and quite placed him in another point of view."

Smelling a small bouquet of half-opened rose-buds which Nugent had presented to her on her taking leave, she continued—" A change of politics in that direction has become a matter of decided expediency; indeed, I may say "—sighing gently—" of clear duty: a mothers duty. Gertrude's maid, Lucy, now an invalid, ascertained through her brother, that Reginald Clinton, the son and heir of old Sir Laurence, was very unwell This at first made no change in my plans, because although I am well aware that Nugent is the next heir, and must come into the property if Reginald Clinton dies, yet the sickness I thought might be no-thing. Yesterday, however, I sent express to the post at Rentworth—Nugent usually waits for his letters to come in the regular course—and received this letter in reply to one I wrote the other day to my dear friend, Emily Hawkshaw, who is staying at the same watering-place as the Clintons—Coppice-on-Shingle. Tis along letter, but the pith of it is in the last sheet."

And she handed it to her husband, who, putting on his spectacles, read with some difficulty as follows:—

PETUNIA LODGE, COPPICE-ON-SHINGLB,

DEAREST LADY MAUD, —

I am delighted, after so long a silence, you should once more drop a line to your faithful Emily. 'Tis ages since you last wrote—I think ftill three years; but the delay only adds to the zest. You ask after me and mine, what I am doing, saying, thinking. 'Tis so kind of you to care about poor me, an emaciated spinster, with friends who frequent Petunia Lodge for the sake of eating my dinners, and relatives who haunt me with a view to being remembered in my will! This place is increasing as fast as it can; castles, villas, Elizabethan halls are studding the hills in a perfect forest. Yes, Coppice-on-Shingle, once a charming solitude, is now disfigured by a crowd of structures, finished and unfinished, in various styles. It looks like an architect's huge lumber-room.

My nieces and I walk as usual three hours a-day. We botanize and pick up shells, a la Sir Isaac Newton. A modest game of whist, or even chess (do not yawn, dearest Lady Maud), is very often our evening amusement. There are not many people of fashion here at this time of year. Four London doctors, thirteen clergymen having something the matter with their throats, several invalids, a few stray dowagers and elderly gentleman, who, under pretence of making love to each other, are perpetually discussing and comparing their respective ailments and infirmities; these are our principal visitors at present. Meantime the sea is very blue, and Puffin's Bay very beautiful, just like some strange unearthly shore Sindbad the sailor might have pitched upon, and perhaps did. The trees are all out in leaf, and have grown much since I last heard from you; but perhaps, with Dr. Johnson, you will rejoin that they have nothing else to do. The pattern for a chair cover you ask for, I enclose, and remain, dearest Lady Maud, always your affectionate friend,

"EMILY HAWKSHAW."

" Why!" exclaimed Mr. Usherwood. " What light does this rigmarole throw on the subject, I should like to know?"

" The postscript—the postscript!" said Lady Maud, and, crossing the end of the letter, there was a postscript discoverable after a little search.

" P.S.—By the bye, I forgot to answer the question you accidentally dropped relative to the Clintons. They *are* here, father and son; the latter in hopeless consumption. I have this moment seen Dr. Pettitoes. He in confidence assured me that Reginald Clinton could not survive a month. The poor old man is much cast down.

"Twill be a good thing for your neighbour the farmer: whom, by the bye, you do not mention."

Mr. Usherwood, after deciphering this important conclusion of the letter, looked up inquiringly to his wife, and seemed still but imperfectly satisfied. Seeing, however, his fair companion's face expressive of gentle triumph, he took a pinch of snuff with some deliberation, as if to clear his intellect, and then observed—

"So, my dear, Reginald Clinton is going to die. Well, and what next?"

" Why, love, I tell you that the Clinton property, although it is not generally known, is strictly entailed, and *must* go to Nugent,"

"Excuse me, but what is the Clinton property? "

"Ten thousand a-year, at least. I have inquired through our London solicitors."

" Reginald was a wild fellow, and gambled terribly," observed her husband dubiously.

" Yes, yes! But the entailed estates, the broad acres, are untouched: they can't move. All the Llannelles-mere property,the Downend andWrexwood-under-River iron mines, the manor of Clinton up in the north, the Chilton-cum-Timsbury estate."

"You seem to have them all at your fingers' ends!"

" I endeavour to do my duty," rejoined her ladyship meekly.

" But why did not you ask him to dinner? "

" My dear, that would be going too fast. We must proceed with delicacy."

"I always rather liked Nugent," Usherwood went on, warming as he proceeded—" I thought he had a sort of superior air about him. In fact, he is a good gentlemanly fellow. 'A fellow that hath had losses,' as Dogberry says. I shall be glad to know more of him."

At this juncture the carriage drove into the park surrounding Beaumont House, and the conversation ceased.

As her ladyship passed along one of the passages leading from the entrance hall, sounds of a piano issuing from an adjacent apartment loudly broke upon her ear. The music was a piece by Thalberg, and brilliantly executed; but occasionally there was that peculiar break-down, followed by an awful pause, which implied the perpetration of a blunder, and the infliction of a scolding. In short, the practice was going on—that exercise by means of which teacher and pupil are very apt to torment each other for a couple of hours at a time, giving and receiving much the same amount of suffering; and ending in an aching heart, red eyes, and a bewildered brain for the rest of the day. So true it is that half mankind seem carefully engaged in tormenting the other half, and receiving precisely the same amount of torment in return. Lady Maud, on hearing the accustomed sounds, turned to her maid who was following her, and said:—

"Paine, be so good as to present my compliments to Miss Beverley, and say I shall be extremely obliged if she will look in upon me whilst I am dressing for dinner."

Miss Beverley was the governess. She had charge of the three Miss Usherwoods. The eldest, Gertrude, was seventeen, and consequently Miss B. was supposed to be finishing her education; imparting, as it were, the last few touches necessary to produce a mellow maturity of polish.

Miss Beverley was a lady of five or six and twenty; a tall and rather handsome brunette, with regular features and sparkling black eyes. She was a good linguist, and a good musician; her reading was little beyond the usual routine of schools, except in the romantic and imaginar-tive line: into this she had latterly flung herself with much fervour, solacing her leisure hours with volumes abstracted from the library, or from Lady Maud's boudoir.

Though somewhat warm in temper, she was well principled, and anxious to do her pupils justice. She gave them whatever information she picked up, in addition to the school-books Lady Maud allowed her; and did not think she had sufficiently secured their spiritual welfare when she had drilled them into repeating the catechism by rote, but gave them as much oral instruction and explanation as her own reading and reflection could supply. She had not had, on the whole, an unhappy time of it. Her pupils, Gertrude, Agatha, and Jessie, though vivacious and a trifle wilful, were kept in order through Lady Maud's influence. Her work was, as it were, cut out for her. She earned her hours of pleasant leisure and her night's rest, at the cost of very moderate exertion. If she was deprived of some of the enjoyments, she was also free from many of the anxieties, of life.

She was far better off than many of her sex, her equals in rank and in means. She was far happier than her cousin Mary, who married the solicitor's clerk in London, and had to bring up seven over-grown children in a small and smoky lodging, and endure the wear and tear of a soured husband who kept late hours. She was more comfortable than her bosom friend Amelia, who ran away with an ensign living on fifty pounds a year and his pay; and, after dawdling away two years in various small towns in the united kingdom, mending her husband's linen, quarrelling with the other officers' wives, and racking her brains to pay her milliner's bill at each change of quarters, was one morning, with her husband and his company, huddled on board an unwieldy trans-port, and duly borne across the Atlantic to the stifling West Indies. She spent a more enjoyable life than her elder sister, who clubbed together with two old maids to live independent and without an object, in an effete watering-place, where she sank into confirmed dyspepsia.

Unfortunately however, Miss Beverley, Lady Maud's governess, a year or two previous to the period we are speaking of, although tolerably happy, doing her duty, and enjoying her music, her books, and her walks, and putting by, out of a salary of a hundred pounds a-year, a handsome portion against future contingencies, attracted the commiseration of one of Lady Maud's visitors, Sir Elliott Prichard, a man of intellect, with profound ideas of human society.

He talked to her eloquently on the grievances of her sex, and especially of that fraction of it who came under the denomination of governess. She listened deferentially, and found out to her surprise that she was a miserable woman. He suggested a course of reading likely to confirm her in a more enlarged view of things in general, and departed; forgetting next day that he had ever seen her in his life. She, however, continued to ruminate on her sad lot, and became liable to occasional low spirits, and an hysterical swelling of the throat. She took in the spirited publication called " Woman's Weekly Witness," and studied a pamphlet entitled ." Pains and Provocations ; or, a Voice from the School-room." She also bought a small octavo volume, purporting to be " The Governess considered in her Social, Scholastic, Political, and Moral Relations." The direct results of this bourse of stimulants were manifested in a rather less even temper; a mournful view of life in general, which approached the maudlin; a vast accession of sensitiveness; a capacity for believing herself slighted when no slight was intended, and fits of romantic desolation, which made herself and others very uncomfortable. For instance, she would go to bed at an extraordinarily early hour, and be wretched all next day because nobody had remarked it. She would glance unutterable things at her pupils, and, when questioned, put her hand to her head, and make no reply. She would sigh deeply without the smallest provocation; and then, abruptly request that nobody would take any notice of her. Nevertheless, her natural good sense and spirits often gained the mastery over these hallucinations, and did not allow her to be utterly spoiled and demoralized: it was a phase of governess experience which could not permanently possess and conquer a good heart and intelligent mind.

Such was Miss Beverley, then, when Paine, tapping at the school-room door, but not putting the smallest fraction of her foot within the room, delivered Lady Maud's message. Leaving her pupil Gertrude to continue her exercise on the piano (which employment that young lady immediately changed for one of Scott's novels), Miss Beverley, smoothing the bands of her black hair, something disordered by the agonies of the music lesson, hastened to Lady Maud's apartments.

Gertrude, after a minute or two, either distracted by her younger sisters, who had deserted their Italian exer-cises and were loud in conversation, pretending to be two ladies of high rank discussing the merits of their respective children—or else carried away by some train of interesting thoughts—dropped the " Heart of Midlothian " into her lap, and sat perfectly motionless before the piano. As the light from a lamp on the chimney-piece fell softly upon her from above, you could see her countenance to the best advantage, and it was certainly one which repaid the trouble of inspection.

She somewhat resembled her mother in the regularity of her features, but her eyes were larger and darker, and shone with a more steady lustre. Her small mouth had an expression of strong determination: an element of the feminine character which is often developed early in life. The hair was a rich brown, Bimply braided, and gathered into a small cap of open crimson net-work, which gave her head a classical appearance. She was of course simply dressed, but wore a small black vel-vet bow to fasten her collar, from which gleamed some valuable jewel. By her place at the table lay the books she had been studying; and near them a vase of choice flowers, and an elegant watch in a case of carved ebony.

She had not sat long in this musing attitude, when a hurried step along the pas-sage announced Miss Beverley's return. Gertrude mechanically struck a few bars on the piano; but Miss Beverley on entering waved her hand, and, in a voice of sup-pressed emotion, desired her to close it; and, on Gertrude evincing hesitation, she sprang to the instrument and slammed it with a loud crash. Whereupon, Gertrude, tossing her head somewhat haughtily, withdrew to the furthest corner of the room, and the two younger ones, much alarmed, commenced writing their exercises with astonishing rapidity.

" All is over!" murmured Miss Beverley, as she went to the window, and looked into the darkness with the dismal earnestness of a Banshee.

"What is the matter, dear Miss Beverley?" asked Gertrude, recovering her good-humour. "What has happened ?"

The other girls kept on writing vigorously, but listened with all their ears. " Nothing—nothing! You will know all soon."

"But tell me, dear—tell me!" continued Gertrude, taking her hand and caressing it.

" Such is life !" exclaimed Miss Beverley in a hoarge whisper. " Gertrude," she added, " your mother, Lady Maud, wishes to see you the moment she leaves the dining-room." She then turned and went hastily to the door, followed by Gertrude. Turning suddenly, she seized her fair pupil by the wrist, and exclaimed With much excitement—" We part I" and, so saying, she van-ished from: the room, and immediately afterwards was heard to lock and bolt her bed-room door with decisive energy. The young ladies gazed in wonder upon each other, and after spending some minutes in whispered but animated conversation, betook themselves to their rooms to dress.

" Gertrude, my sweet child," said her mother, " sit beside me on the sofa."

That young lady in some agitation seated herself, whilst her mother, taking her hand affectionately, began to criticise and alter the minutiae of her daughter's costume. "My dear creature, what a figure you are! Let me smooth your hair. Your collar is quite crooked. I wish that poor Lucy of yours would get better, or that you would give her up, and find another maid."

" Mamma, I should be sorry to forsake her in her misfortune."

"My love, your feeling on the subject is much to your credit. But, if she refuses to get better, what is to be done? Is it worth while to keep the place vacant for her?"

"Well, mamma, she is an excellent servant, so kind, and civil, and well-be-haved—quite a pattern ladies' maid! "

"Paine says she is pert and inquisitive."

"That means that she is younger, prettier, and cleverer than herself."

"My dear," said her mother, "I desired Miss Beverley to request you to come to me, as I have something to say to you. Put your arm round my waist, dear. The fact is, Gertrude, on mature reflection, I have decided to take you out of the school-room; and, in short, introduce you to society."

Gertrude turned crimson with surprise and pleasure.

"Ah! you must learn a few things yet, my dear, though you have left the school-room. You must ac-quire composure, gentleness, command of countenance. That will do, love, your kisses are too vivacious; my dress is in disorder." Lady Maud stopped to restore her toilette to its wonted perfection, and then proceeded: " You speak French as well as can be expected for an un-travelled Englishwoman, Italian passably. German you can read, I believe; I am pleased with your execution on the piano, and with your singing; further I don't know much about your acquirements, but I have confi-dence in Miss Beverley."

There was a pause, and mother and daughter sat with their arms encircling each other's waist, pursuing for a moment the current of their own reflections.

"You will now, of course, dine with us, dear, and accompany us in our calls, and visits, and gaieties, such as they are in this secluded corner of the world. Your allowance will be increased, and I shall write at once to town to Madame Alphonse to take your toilette in hand. It would be well if you read a few books of general information. The Quarterly Review, Bowdler's Shak-8peare, some books of Trav-els—your father and I will look out a few. And I should like you to read some useful works: for example—Mrs. Loudon's' Gardening for Ladies, and her Country

Companion. And another nice book I know,'Every Lady her own Dairymaid,' in one volume.*

" I will do all you wish, dearest mamma."

" And here, love, is a small token of regard," added her mother, taking a small box from an adjacent work-table. It contains jewels: some of them your late lamented great-grandmother's, the Counters of Delaffield; some new: they are all I think prettily set and arranged. Embrace me, my love. And, by the bye, I had forgotten an illuminated Prayer-Book, of which I beg your acceptance."

It was elaborately got up. Three bright blue convolvuli and a sprig of myrtle twisted round the margin of each page in violent convulsions. The capital letters shone like a blaze of fireworks. It was what is called a Sunday Service Book. The Psalms for morning and evening being placed in different parts of the book, and other alterations made, confusing to any unfortunate into whose hands it falls for the first time during divine service: for, with a countenance growing redder and redder, he vainly endeavours to find his place, and at last lays the book down in despair, at the risk of being thought by the congregation to be either an obdurate Dissenter or partially blind.

Gertrude was all gratitude, and commenced ransacking her jewels, and commenting on them one by one.

" Oh, I wish Miss Beverley was here!" she cried.

"Well, why does she not come? She knows she is always welcome."

"Oh, she has gone to her room, and locked the door!"

" Positively it is dangerous to one's health!" said Lady Mady; "I foresee another scene."

" Shall I take her some tea, mamma ? "

" Yes, any thing—every thing."

Gertrude was hastening out of the room with a cup of tea, when Lady Maud exclaimed—

"By the bye, Gertrude, has Lucy Weston every thing she wants ? "

" We left word you know, mamma, that she was to send for whatever she fancied, but she has only sent once for some currant jelly. I cannot help fearing, the housekeeper must have been cross, or something of the kind."

"Well, my dear—I think it would be a kind and right thing if you were to call on her yourself, and take a little basket of comforts for the poor girl."

" Oh, I should like it above all things! When may I go, mamma ? "

" To-morrow, dear, if you like, at about twelve o'clock, But be careful not to go into the cottage. There may be infection."

Gertrude now pursued her way to Miss Beverley's apartment. But that lady, after sitting on the rug opposite the fireless grate, for some minutes in total darkness, had gradually come to the conclusion that she should find her situation pleasanter at the tea-table, with a lighted candle and a well-furnished tray before her. Accordingly she had waylaid a wandering house-maid, and signified her wishes, and, not being unpopular amongst the domestics, was very soon provided with lights and refreshment. She was about half-way through her solitary meal, and was reading, for the third time, that valuable pamphlet, " Pains and Provocations; or, a Voice from the School-room," which she had propped up against the sugar-basin, when a gentle tap was heard at the door, and a voice asking if she would take a cup of tea. Miss Beverley's face immediately assumed the Banshee expression, and, taking care not to rattle the tea-things, she answered in a sepulchral voice—"No, Gertrude—no, I want no tea: do not mind me." Gertrude inquired if she might come in;.but Miss Beverley, having just taken a mouthful of buttered toast, thought it more prudent as well as decorous to preserve silence, and Gertrude began slowly to walk away.

Miss Beverley's better feelings, however, now prevailed, and, springing to the door, she flung it open and exclaimed—

" Gertrude dear, I have tea, hot-buttered toast, and an egg—come in!"

The next moment they were embracing each other, and shedding tears with that promptitude peculiar to the fair sex. Then, sitting down, they discussed the remainder of the tea and buttered toast, and talked over Gertrude's change of position and prospects.

" Well," said Gertrude, " I dare say I shall find my time hang heavy enough on my hands, now I have done with lessons."

" Oh!" rejoined her companion, "all will be novelty to you; you will enjoy your liberty immensely. I shall find the school-room very dull without you. You will have new friends, new associations—I shall be no one!" and Miss Beverley was in danger for a moment of elapsing into despondency.

"Don't say so," said Gertrude, taking her hand; " we will be friends all the same, and read books, and play duets, and sketch together, and you shall give me a good scolding now and then, as of old, to keep up your spirits."

Miss Beverley smiled at her former pupil, with her eyes brimful of tears.

"And," continued Gertrude, "we will walk together, and you shall talk to me of the past, and tell me some of those romantic stories you used to favour me with when we had had a good day. Why, where am I to find friends and new associations hereabouts, I should like to know? There's no one really but two or three clergymen, and Sir Eliot Prichard, and the great coal-mine proprietor, and two or three distant squires."

" You forget Mr. Nugent at the Manor-house."

"The Manor-house Farm, you should call it, my dear," rejoined Gertrude.

"It's a most mysterious place!" exclaimed the romantic governess. " Depend upon it, there are some strange old stories about that house, and about the Nugents, and the ruins, and the old avenue. I shouldn't be at all surprised if the rick barton was not haunted by a ghost!" she added, with some solemnity.

" I cannot see any thing romantic in a farm-yard," answered Gertrude.

" But, my dear, consider. Years ago, before you or I were born, when those tall elms were thin, fragile, tender saplings, there stood, no doubt, a grand old picturesque mansion in the centre of those park-like grounds. Doubtless the Nugents were wont, in those days, to issue forth with their armed retainers, and strike a gallant stroke for altar and for crown."

" Pm afraid they were Puritans !" exclaimed Gertrude, laughing.

 " Well, then, for freedom and for faith!" replied Miss Beverley, rapidly adjusting her romantic visions to the exigencies of prosaic history.

"Wounded knights," she continued, "have been borne bleeding up that avenue, lovely damsels have climbed the hill, to watch for father, or brother, or lover returning from the wars. Oh, depend upon it, it is a mysterious place! I do hope Mr. Nugent will some day recover his position, re-purchase all his ancestral estates, and be M.P. for the county, High Sheriff and Lord-Lieutenant into the bargain! I think him so interesting! He always looks as if he were somebody who, for excellent reasons, thought it expedient to wear a temporary disguise."

"My dear, how excited you are! Now, just look at these beautiful jewels mamma has given me. Is it not kind?"

As soon as due admiration had been lavished on her presents, that young lady bade Miss Beverley good-night, and hurried away to her bed-room. Here, seemingly disinclined for going to rest, she occupied herself with arranging the room afresh, altering the situation of chairs and tables, changing books, distributing her ornaments in new situations. There was over the mantelpiece a picture of a Madonna (a small copy of a Guido), and before it was placed an elegant little marble figure of Flora, scattering flowers round her. Gertrude took away the picture, and hung it in another part of the room, placing a copy of Beatrice Cenci in its place Then she removed the Flora, and placed instead of it her new illuminated prayer-book, with two alabaster Cupids playing together on one side, and on the other a stuffed bullfinch under a glass case, trying to catch a faded butterfly. She seemed pleased with this arrangement, and completed the effect by a vase of flowers at each end of the mantelpiece. She then, with a certain degree of impetuosity not unusual in her, proceeded to the bookcase, and, glancing her eye over a row of school-books of slightly invalided aspect, seized at least two-thirds of them, one after another, and piling them in the grate, set them on fire, encouraging the conflagration by a copious libation of wax from her bed-room candles.

After gazing with much satisfaction at this literary bonfire, she hastened to her writing-table, and re-plenished her blotting-book by two quires of best Bath post, and a quire of cream-tinted note-paper; arranging pens and sealing-wax in proportion in the inkstand adjacent. She then decked herself in the whole of the jewels lately presented to her by her mother, and stood before the looking-glass investigating her appearance for about ten minutes. At length an expression of weariness began to settle upon that pretty face, mingled with self-reproach, and, taking off her ornaments, she rang for her maid, or rather for her mother's maid. That worthy woman, however, after waiting in the housekeeper's room till half-past eleven, in expectation of the young lady's bell—passing the time in grumbling against all young ladies in general, and in little uneasy dozes and fragmentary slumbers-having twice set her cap on fire, had retired bodily to bed, and was sleeping, as Sydney Smith would say, with "forty housemaid power." Consequently, Gertrude rang in vain, and at length, with the air of a martyr, undressed herself, and succeeded in getting safely to bed without assistance.

CHAPTER III.

THE TWO PRISONERS.

Miss BEVERLEY was not fax from the truth in assuming that Nugent's ancestors had been great people in their day. They had owned the land which he now rented, and a great many broad acres besides. Once an old manorial residence rose in varied but picturesque proportions upon the gentle slope of that wooded hillside, towards which the avenue of elms, already described, formed a stately approach. Some heavy fines, inflicted for political offences under the agreeable regime of the Stewarts, followed up by an inroad of the sea, which carried havoc over the low lands in the district, had shaken the stability and curtailed the resources of the family. The property was burdened with mortgage after mortgage, until the owners were little better than collectors of rent for the benefit of expectant creditors.

When Nugent's father succeeded to the possessions of his ancestors, he found himself nothing better than a penniless gentleman, surrounded by an empty pageant of hill and dale, rich meadow and productive arable, the rent of which he never touched, and a fine old house decaying for want of repairs, which he could scarcely afford to keep warm and habitable. Early scenes of anxiety, and of bitter humiliation, had somewhat soured his mind, but at the same time infused into him a wholesome austerity and practical vigour suitable to his circumstances. His great aim and secret ambition was by degrees, however slowly, yet at some time or other, to pay off the debts which crippled and crushed the estate, and to come forth once more an independent man. This object filled his whole soul. He had seen the debasing misery of debt, the petty shifts, the effort to keep up a show of luxury and ease, the abject dependence on unworthy confidants and auxiliaries, the aching cares, and the half-unconscious trickery to which men, by no means of low average honesty, oftentimes descend, when they owe more than they can pay, and yet keep up an establishment which continually increases the amount of what they owe, whilst it diminishes their ability of discharging it. He strove hard, therefore, to conquer the difficulties bequeathed to him. It was a severe and trying struggle. In the midst of it an accident happened, which at first sight appeared disastrous, but proved most beneficial. The Manor-house, in his absence from home, was set on fire through the carelessness of a servant, and completely gutted by the flames; which fed voraciously on its old wainscots and well-dried timbers, its roof of Spanish chestnut, its floors of polished oak. He was for a couple of hours prostrated by the accumulated misfortunes which beset him. But his strong spirit speedily rallied. His resolution was soon taken. Some kind friends and relations urged the rebuilding of his house in its ancient style, at any cost or sacrifice. He inquired drily how much they would contribute towards the work, and was very shortly left alone to his own reflections. He drew from the quarter where he had invested them, half the savings of several years' steady self-denial and frugality. He employed this sum in completing the destruction of his house, and in erecting, on the site of the old stables, the unpretending abode we have briefly described. He altered and added to the various offices around it. Finally, he took into his own. hands a few hundred acres convenient to the house, and turned farmer in sober earnest.

The trials and difficulties of his progress through life, drove him to seek support and comfort from the exercise of religious faith. His tone of mind, and indeed the hereditary principles of his family, imparted somewhat of a rigid and narrow character to his religious views. He was a puritan, but also an honest servant of God, and derived abundant consolation and hope from the truth which he had embraced, and to which he faithfully adhered throughout a long and busy life. Meantime, he worked at his farm with a kind of stern, resolute enthusiasm.

The needy squire began to be transformed into the thriving yeoman. He married a lady young, handsome, and well educated; for a lady, poor—for a farmer's wife, tolerably well off. Her sweet and gentle disposition softened the harshness of her husband's temper, and mitigated its natural austerity. When Oliver their only son grew up to man's estate, the old man summoned him into his private room, and explained to him the whole state of the family affairs; described all the trials and humiliations he himself had undergone; and put it to him whether he would prefer to sneak and shuffle through life as a pauper gentleman, or look the best man in the realm boldly in the face as an upright, independent yeoman?

Oliver's choice was soon made. The fether and son cut off the entail of the still burdened estate; sold the whole of it, except about 600 acres immediately around the house; with the proceeds, and the accumulated savings of some years, liquidated every farthing of debt; and then, with hearts light and joyous, settled down on the unembarrassed property, now in every sense their own, and continued to farm it with activity and success.

Anticipating the possibility of his son's gaining a higher position in society than he himself had bequeathed to him, he thought it right that Oliver should have an excellent education: such an education as should amply accord with any future improvement in his worldly circumstances. He should not indeed send him to either of the universities; but a lew yeans at a public school, and a year or two with an excellent tutor, proved amply sufficient for the object in view.

Three years only had elapsed since the death of Oliver's parents, at the period when the present narrative commences; but, for some time before his father's decease, Nugent had assumed and carried on the management of the small estate now belonging to his family.

In addition to the freehold property, he rented two or three hundred acres of adjacent land, once his father's, but since passed into the hands of strangers.

The management of a farm of this extent requires much experience, ability, and vigour. The mind of the agriculturist must be capable of forming, as each year revolves, plans of multitudinous detail; embracing the operations of the field; the rotation of crops; the treatment of each particular piece of land; the sale and purchase of stock and produce; the economy of the stable, the stall, the sheepfold, &c.; and a multitude of other matters.

Meantime a careful eye must be fixed upon the fluctuations of the market; and a vigilant and energetic supervision extended over the numerous labourers and workmen employed in the field or in the yard; from the bailiff to the boy who scares the birds from the wheat; from the head carter to the old woman who strips the leaves from the turnips previous to their being thrown into the turnip-crusher.

Fortitude, patience, self-command, a cool judgment, even we may add courage, are required when the time of harvest draws near; and over-precipitation on the one hand, or too timid and hesitating a step on the other, may inflict disastrous losses on the fanner, and render vain the toil and anxiety of many months. It is a pleasant and a wholesome spectacle to see any one amidst such trials and difficulties preserve a manly cheerfulness of demeanour; maintain an even temper under varying circumstances; and rise with renewed vigour after every check and disappointment.

Nugent was calm and steady, if he was not light-hearted and buoyant. His voice might not impart a gay fearlessness to his men, but it braced them to resolute perseverance. Quiet confidence, invincible endurance, and at all times a simple spirit of resignation, coupled with a cautious yet enterprising temper, fore-sight, and self-command, these were Nugent's principal characteristics as an agriculturist. The daily authority he exercised over BO many around him, acting upon a mind by nature inclined to be self-sufficing and confident in its own conclusions, had gradually wrought in him a habit of setting too low a value on the opinions of others when they differed from his own. He examined a matter honestly and earnestly, and, when he had once made up his mind upon it, felt some difficulty in believing that, after all, he might be mistaken. In practice he often gave up his opinion; but when he succumbed it was rather in the spirit of a martyr than of a convert. His judgments were generally just and true from his own point of view; but he did not always make allowance for the almost inevitable prejudices and predilections of others, nor take into calculation the possible inaccuracy of his own deductions, and the bias of his own mind. He was strongly and sincerely under the influence of religion. A little of a puritan, he was nevertheless a fairly loyal servant of the Church of England. Some portions of her doctrine and formularies he might object to; on others he might harbour doubts; but these were exceptional points of disagreement. He valued, obeyed, and to a certain degree reverenced, his church as a whole. A respect for discipline and order, an abhorrence of wrangling and confusion, were strong motives to retain him in a society in which the truth was substantially taught, even if it were occasionally infected by error: a society containing in its ranks so many excellent and pious men, and extending over the length and breadth of the land a wholesome and salutary influence.

The day after Lady Maud's visit to the Manor-house Farm, Nugent, just returned from his usual ride over the estate, threw the reins of his strong active galloway to one of his men, and, entering the house, proceeded to a long low room which went by the name of the library; although, to say the truth, the few shelves, and those seantily provided with books, ranged round the room, did not impart to it a very literary aspect.

You descended into it by three steps, and as the ceiling was of dark oak boards crossed by heavy horizontal ribs of the same material, remnants of the ancient mansion, the first impression received was not lively. The latticed window was indeed broad, but the level of the floor being below the external ground, much light was not admitted; especially when the roses and honeysuckles had made their summer shoots, and hung over and beset the window on all sides, as if struggling to force their way in. The chimneypiece was composed of fragments of carved stone; two massive blocks on each side supporting a slab of sandstone, under which two or three corbels were inserted—weather-beaten faces of an unearthly expression, whose grim but yet dignified severity was not softened by a slight stain of smoke arising from their proximity to the fire. The furniture of the room was of a plain, almost meagre description. The walls were covered with a cheap and sickly-looking paper; green baize covered the floor. Over the old chimneypiece hung the portrait of a lady of middle age, of a sweet and serious cast of countenance, and a quiet nobility of aspect.

There was a cupboard full of papers and account-books, and against one side of the room a gun or two, a brace of pistols, a hunting-whip, and three ancient swords of the dates respectively of Agincourt, the Armada, and the Commonwealth, were suspended. Whilst the remaining walls were ornamented by an agricultural almanac mounted map-like on a roller, a handsome barometer, a portrait of a favourite horse, a coloured drawing of various fungi and insects hostile to the growth of plants, five walking-sticks of various shapes and sizes, and a few book shelves. On the chimney-piece were two or three small canvass bags containing samples of grain or seed, a small model of a drilling-machine, an antique snuff-box filled with copper caps, and a small paper parcel containing a specimen of superphosphate of lime. The books on the shelves were principally on agricultural subjects, but there were a few works of general instruction. There was also a Greek Testament, Virgil's Georgics, Hesiod, two gigantic folios reposing one atop of the other (one of them Scott's Commentary, the other a Greek Lexicon), besides a heap of dusty pamphlets, tracts, and venerable newspapers.

Nugent entered this room, sat down to the table, pulled a large desk towards him, and, placing his watch on one side of it, commenced writing two or three letters. Now and then he glanced at his watch, and, when the hour-hand approached eleven, he rose, sealed and directed his letters, and dropped them into a small leathern case, which he placed outside the door. One of the letters was addressed to Sir Laurence Clinton, Bart., The Grotto, Coppice-on-Shingle; and we take the liberty of briefly mentioning the contents. They were expressive of sympathy, unaffected but cordial, with the old man on account of the dangerous illness of his beloved son, who, a few months before, was one of the handsomest and gayest habitués of Paris and Florence; but now, a weak and wasted invalid, with hollow cheeks and dreamy eye, he was drawn about in a bath-chair on sunny days up and down the esplanade, his old fether walking by his side and occasionally holding his hand.

It was a delicate matter for any man to write a letter of condolence on an affliction which might produce so ' great a change for the better in his own circumstances; but Nugent did not feel any embarrassment: he was simple and direct in what he took in hand; was not vehemently interested in the possible effects Reginald Clinton's death might have upon his worldly fortunes, but sincerely grieved for the distracted father; and wrote accordingly.

After giving some directions to one or two men who were waiting for him outside, he took his hat and stick, and, going through the garden, walked at a quick pace
up the sloping lawn upon which the drawing-room looked out, and passed through
a gate at the upper end, · under some tall fir-trees. From thence he was soon upon
a breezy down, which overlooked his whole farmstead and the broad valley to the
left, and on the right gave a fine view of the broad, ever-changing sea. He pursued
his way along the down for some distance; occasionally passing between clumps of
gorse glowing with yellow blossoms, stunted hollies green and hardy, and twisted thorn-bushes bent all awry, and throwing out in one direction their crooked
branches, as if to escape from the prevalent wind which vexed them.

After stopping to converse with his shepherd—whom he found, not playing
on a pipe, but unrotaantically devouring bread and cheese on the lee side of a wall,
with some hundred sheep cropping the short herbage around him—Nugent turned
down a precipitous path, that conducted him to an angle of the valley, along which
an irregular road wound, flanked on one side by pollard ash and an occasional thin
and meagre fir-tree; interspersed with thatched cottages of ancient aspect, their
gables sometimes turned towards the road, sometimes at right angles. On the other
side an arable field stretched; upon which three ploughs were busily at work.

This hamlet once belonged to the Nugents, but had long since come into other
hands. Small as it appeared to be, three beer-shops were conspicuous at intervals
along the road, exhibiting, through the dirty panes of their lower window, a row
of pewter pots smeared with the dregs of the stupefying beer or poisonous cider
which the owners retailed to their customers. The cottages seemed, many of them,
out of repair and neglected by the landlord; but in some there was an air of neatness and order, and an attempt at ornament within and ·without, rather cheering
to witness.

Nugent stopped at one or two of them, and entering in remained there a few
minutes.

It had been for some time his habit to visit the sick and poor of his parish. He did this partly from a kind and charitable feeling; partly because, as an overseer and churchwarden, he felt a satisfaction in ascertaining that the poorand the sick were duly provided for, and that the ratepayer's interests were at the same time honestly protected. Although, therefore, in the main actuated by Christian motives, there was an intermixture of business-like vigilance, which might have given him, in the eyes of a stranger, the aspect rather of a hard-headed parish officer looking after the interests of the public, than of a kind-hearted, yet prudent, friend of the needy and suffering; as Nugent really was. The poor, whom he frequently succoured, and the sick, whom he watched over and provided for as if they were per-sonal friends, did not always feel that glow of affection-ate gratitude which might have been expected. His manner was reserved; he had not the best method of comforting or advising the suffering and the erring. Many, however, loved him, and all respected, even whilst they feared him."

After paying visits, then, to a few poor people, Nugent proceeded along the main road for a little distance until he came to a solitary cottage, with a thatched roof green with moss, in the midst of a good-sized but thoroughly neglected garden. The window of the ground floor room bad a broken pane, in which a battered old hat had been carelessly stuffed. He opened the ricketty little gate leading into the garden, and walked up to the cottage along a path ankle-deep in weeds.

He knocked, but receiving no answer, or at least hearing none, tried to open the door, but found it locked. As he heard the noise of children inside he knocked again, but still no notice was taken. He then looked through the window, removing for the purpose the old hat just mentioned. Upon a bed, against one of the walls of the small room, lay the form of a woman greatly reduced by sickness. She was not old, but was evidently very ill. There was no article of furniture in the room except this bed, and an empty deal box which seemed to be used as a table. The bed was old and worm-eaten; but a new and substantial blanket or two, with decent sheets, enveloped the sick woman. Two or three young children, pale and in rags, were engaged in violent play, rolling about on the stone floor of the cottage. By the poor woman's side lay a thick ash twig, and occasionally, as the children came within reach, she would bid them be quiet, and at the same time seize the stick, and with a feverish effort strike at them. The little ones, thus admonished, would scramble out of reach of their mother's arm, and for a few moments cease their clamour, only to commence presently with fresh vigour.

Nugent gazed for a few minutes on this painful scene with a look of anxiety and sorrow, as if grieving over what he saw, and reflecting how he might best put a stop to it. Suddenly the children perceived him, and all slunk into different corners of the room, and one into the deal box. He spoke to the sick mother.

"Mrs. Harrill—Margaret, how do you feel to-day?"

"Main bad, Squire Nugent," answered the woman. " I have no peace."

"I cannot get the door open," continued Nugent.

"O dear!" said the woman, "you see I sent Edward out for a loaf, and he locks the door, or may be the bairns would get into the road and be run over.

"I fear they disturb you."

"I can't say but they do that, Squire Nugent. Only, when Edward's at home he keeps them quiet enough, but when he goes out they're all wild-like again." And the poor woman shook her stick feebly at the young "urchin in the deal box, who was peeping out at "the gentleman."

" And how does Edward go on?" asked Nugent.

" Oh! for the matter of that, he eats hearty; and he'll be a good strapping lad by and bye."

"But how do you like him? Is he useful to you? Does he behave well?"

" He is a blessing to me," said the woman earnestly. " I should have been dead before now if it hadn't been along of him."

" Let us see—you receive a shilling a week from the parish?"

" Yes, your honour—and it's too little. Pm not in power able to do with it: I'm not, indeed!"

" My good woman, don't say so. 'Tis more than you have a right to expect. But here is Edward."

And a boy of about ten years old, carrying on one shoulder a quartern-loaf, entered the little garden. He was a slim and handsome child, with a thoughtful but almost gloomy countenance, and deep black eyes. He looked hard at Nugent, and then put his hand to his cap. Opening the door of the cottage he went in, followed by Nugent, and, placing the loaf on the box, was immediately surrounded by all the children, whose eager looks showed that they were now any thing but disposed to play. The boy produced a large pocket-knife, and began cutting the loaf into equal slices; reserving a piece of the crumb for the sick woman. Whilst the boy was gravely, and with strict justice, distributing the bread to the anxious claimants around him, Nugent conversed] in a' low voice with [the mother.

"You have not heard from anyone about the boy then?"

" No, sir, not a word. Who's to care, sir, about such as he ? He's a love child, and no one will claim him."

"But how do you know ? "

" The poor lady owned it to Harrill afore she died, at least so Harrill says: but he don't much like to talk of her, and would swear awful if I questioned him."

" You say Harrill used to get plenty of money from some quarter or other when you first came here ?"

" Plenty for all of us!" exclaimed the woman, flushing with shame and excitement; "but that wicked man wasted it shameful."

"At the beer-shop !"

"Ay, ay!—the most of it went that way, as the most of it goes now."

"Well," rejoined Nugent, "you have acted a kind part by the boy."

" I will do so as long as I have life left me; but 'tis he looks after me now. I should be dead were it not for he."

" You would be for better in the work-house than in this wretched place: no quiet; no comfort."

The woman shook her head emphatically. " I can't abide to lose my children: I have 'em here all day about me; and it's cheerful-like, you see. And then there's Ned; I couldn't part with Ned."

The poor woman now showed symptoms of hysterics, and Nugent thought best to drop his favourite topic of conversation with her—the advantages of the work-house over her present miserable abode.

" Is your husband kinder now ? " he asked.

" Much the same. He let me keep the blankets your honour sent, but he changed away one of the sheets for drink."

Nugent's countenance darkened. "I tell you what, Margaret, this must not continue. You had relief last week from the Board; your husband is able to keep you off the parish if he chose to work; and I shall pull him up at the next Justice meeting, and give him another month in the county jail. He knows the way there now."

Tears came into the woman's sunken eyes, but she was too fatigued to say much more; and Nugent, after a few kind words of encouragement, rose from the edge of the bed where he had been sitting, put a packet of tea and sugar into the boy Edward's hand, with a tract for him to read to Margaret, and then, shaking her by the hand, departed.

He now struck across the fields until he reached the main road which intersected the valley, along which he proceeded about a mile, until he came in sight of a handsome country seat surrounded by extensive pleasure-grounds, and a park which seemed to have been recently composed by throwing several fields into one.

Young trees were planted about in groups, fenced in various ways to protect them against sheep and cattle; a belt of young plantation, still too diminutive to overstep the palings placed in front of it—fir, larch, beech, oak, all huddled together, struggling for air and elbow-room—lined one side of the park.

Nugent's eye wandered for a moment to the distant house. Little accustomed to artifice, he did not attribute Lady Maud's change of conduct towards him to any selfish motives. He thought her capricious and changeable, but, on the whole, was glad of the sort of amende she had made him.

Not far from the lodge which formed the entrance into the park, two or three cottages were situated. To one of these Nugent directed his steps. It was a decent-looking cottage, with a large window looking into the road. This window contained a printed placard, announcing the fact that George Weston, "Medical Professor and Scientific Herbalist," might be consulted daily from ten till four, and giving a long list of diseases that he professed to cure by means of the simple remedies which long experience and extensive familiarity with botany had suggested to him. " Consulting fee, two shillings and sixpence. N.B.—Money returned if no relief afforded. *Mens sana in corpore sano?* The Latin quotation was a masterly stroke of policy, and had conquered the scepticism of many a country bumpkin, after he had for many days together flattened his nose against the window frame as he returned home from work, and marvelled whether the quack-doctor could do any thing for " our Polly," or for the " old woman," or for " little Tommy."

In addition to these medical announcements, there were one or two advertisements of a somewhat different character. For example:—a half sheet of paper contained samples of elaborate penmanship, with an intimation under that George Weston wrote letters on any subject—whether to distant relatives and sweethearts, or to persons of rank and authority, from members of parliament down to guardians of the poor—at the moderate charge of twopence a sheet. Furthermore, there was a notice that George Weston purposed delivering his usual monthly lecture at the "Red Lion," at the hour of seven o'clock in the evening, on Monday next. "Subject— Evenings with the Necessarians; or, was Greenacre a murdered man? Ad-mission, one penny."

At the door of this cottage Nugent knocked, and the door was presently opened by Weston himself, the man mentioned in our first chapter, with his coat off and an open Bible in his hand.

" How is Lucy ! " inquired Nugent.

" Very weak, sir. Quite prostrate. Never saw her so bad. She has no more strength than a baby." And the man passed the sleeve of his shirt across his eyes.

"You see, Mr. Nugent," he continued, "I'm too deeply interested to prescribe for her myself. I have called in Mr. Grierson, and he visits her daily. But he don't deny there's danger."

"Well," observed Nugent, "I am glad you have a book in your hand which is our best companion in trouble. Do you read it to her? "

"Ay, sir, every day. She says it does her good. And I believe it's a first-rate book for a sick-room, it's so full of comforting thoughts; though you know, Mr. Nugent,

I am unable to admit its inspiration, and question its authenticity into the bargain." Nugent looked deeply offended, and said—

" I have no authority over you—none whatever. But at least, for your sister's sake, forbear to speak slightingly of the revealed word of God—of that God in whose hands your sister now is."

" Sir, I meant no offence," answered Weston; "I have a great respect for a portion of the Scriptures: you really misunderstand me."

Nugent said no more, but asked to see his sister, and climbed up the stairs to the small bed-room above.

He found Lucy in a very low state, scarcely able to speak, and soon took leave of her, after kindly pressing her hand. As he descended the precipitous stairs, he heard confused but earnest whispers below.

" I tell you he is up-stairs, coming down this very moment; you must go!"

" George—be easy; be easy," replied a voice somewhat indistinct in its utterance. " I'm all right: I say I'm all right. Give us a light, and a drink of something cool."

"Go, I say!" urged Weston. Just then Nugent alighted in the room, and beheld a rough-looking, strong-built man, who, resisting the efforts of Weston, had seated himself by the fire, and sticking his pipe into the coals, commenced puffing tobacco-smoke from his mouth and nostrils in huge volumes. Recognizing in this half-drunken visitor Jack Harrill, the husband of Margaret, Nugent looked at him with grave displeasure. The man, slowly comprehending who it was that was looking at him, sat in stupid perplexity. " Put out that light!" exclaimed Nugent; " there is a sick woman upstairs."

" The smoke will hurt your sister," he added, turning to Weston, who was regarding Harrill with the strongest disgust, but nevertheless did not interfere.

After a moment's delay, the man seemed suddenly to understand what was passing, and who spoke to him. He jumped up and bolted out of the house, muttering a curse between his teeth.

"So," said Nugent, "you still cling to your mischievous associates. Is it for such friendship as that of this fellow Harrill, that you have sacrificed my friendship and good-will ? Can you find any compensation for the ruin of your prospects in associating with a notorious drunkard, or in spouting sedition at beer-shops, or in still worse employments?" Nugent added, pointing to a soiled pack of cards, which Harrill had left on the chair where he had been sitting.

" l am the victim of circumstances," answered Weston in a low voice, whilst he pressed his hand to his brow.

It is our habit pretty constantly to lay the blame of our follies or misdeeds upon " circumstances:" it is a large, vague, convenient phrase. What Nugent would have replied we know not, for at that moment a sudden scream for assistance interrupted their conversation. " Is it Lucy ? " cried Nugent. "No," said the other; "it was in the road, outside." They rushed out of the cottage, and saw, about a hundred yards down the road, a young lady, in much terror and distress, endeavouring to escape from the man Harrill, who, whether in earnest or sottish jest, strove to possess himself of a small flat basket she was carrying on her arm. This would have been a very easy matter; but the strings of the basket were entangled round her wrist, and she was thus not only unable to extricate herself from his grasp, but was suffering real pain from the violent efforts he made to pull the basket away from her. Nugent shouted loudly to the man to let go his hold, and at the same time sprang towards him with a menacing gesture.

His energy was not diminished on perceiving that the young lady was no other than Gertrude.

The man immediately let go the basket, and turning full upon Nugent, his face crimson with rage and excite-ment, yelled out—

" Yes,yes—thou'rt the man that sneaked to my house this morning, and wants to clap me in quod again! In for a penny, in for a pound. So, here goes!" with which he seized a stone to fling at Nugent; but, ere he could do so, Nugent's strong hand had got him by the throat. The man was inflamed but not disabled by liquor; and his brute strength would have been formidable to an antagonist less resolute and less powerful than Nugent. A few seconds of fierce struggle, the two men swinging each other about the road amidst a cloud of dust; and then Harrill lay panting on his back, and Nugent kneeling on his chest to keep him down.

Gertrude, at first too frightened to do or say any thing, ran to the lodge for aid. Now, the old lodge-keeper had in fact been watching the encounter from his bed-room window; but prudently waited until Nugent had got the upper hand before taking a decided part in the engagement. He hastily anticipated Gertrude's appeal, and issued forth from his den with an air of great determination, and armed with an aged gun, which might have been a formidable weapon if it had possessed a lock.

" Andrew! Help! Quick! Do you mean to let us be murdered in cold blood ? "

"I'm a coming, miss," replied the old man. "Don't be afeard. I'll pertect ye—I'll pertect ye!"

Weston, hearing Nugent calling him, now emerged from his cottage, where he also had remained quietly ensconced during the contest.

" Here, help me to hold this fellow, some of you. Where have you been ? Why did you not stand by me ? " exclaimed Nugent.

" Lucy was frightened, and called me back. She was nearly off in a faint."

Harrill meanwhile began to growl out assurances that he gave in, that 'twas all a joke, that he was main sorry, and promised to be as quiet as a lamb. Nugent therefore suffered him to rise, having taken the precaution of pinioning his arms with some rope which the old man procured.

He then turned to Gertrude with an air of anxious concern, and asked her whether she was not hurt and frightened.

That young lady, now that the moment of excitement had passed, was indeed pale and exhausted, and felt as if a good cry would do her good. But she repressed her tears, and, taking Nugent's arm, accepted his escort home. Harrill was left at the lodge, in charge of Weston and the old man.

" Pray, tell me," said Nugent, " how this unfortunate affair began."

" Mamma sent me into the village," began Gertrude, " to visit a poor person."

"Your maid Lucy, no doubt?" interposed Nugent, whilst his countenance exhibited real pleasure at the thought of Gertrude's recollection of her.

"Yes," replied Gertrude, slightly blushing, for she knew she had forgotten, or not thought it necessary, to call for nearly a week. " I was going to ask after Lucy, and give her some little comforts the housekeeper put into that basket for me. I generally send one of the maids," she honestly added; for she did not relish unmerited praise, "To-day I went myself, partly because momma wished it, partly because I was really anxious about the poor thing. Well, just as I got outside the lodge gates, that fierce-looking man came and stood right in my way, and proposed I should give him something to drink. I thought he had had too much already, and tried to run back to the lodge; but he seized my basket, declaring it was too heavy for me to carry. Then the string got twisted round my hand, and he pulled and pulled, and could not get it away, and, searching with his other hand in his pocket for a knife, swore he would have the basket if he had to cut off my arm for it. I had not screamed till that moment, but then I screamed louder than I ever did in my life, and, to my inexpressible delight, I saw you come out of that cottage, and rush to my assistance!"

" I wish the fellow had never come into the place. We must try and get rid of him."

" You are very pale, sir," said Gertrude, looking compassionately at Nugent. " I hope you are not hurt."

" Oh, it's nothing—nothing I" rejoined her companion. "Do you know, Miss Usherwood, why it is that Lucy's brother, George Weston, is so intimate with a coarse ruffianly fellow like Harrill ? it seems very strange."

"Lucky is so mysterious about her brother," answered Gertrude. " She never likes his name to be mentioned, and yet she seems tenderly attached to him. I have heard her say her brother hates Harrill, and thinks him a desperately bad character; so I was all the more alarmed when you called out that name in the struggle just now—for I did not know till then who it was."

"And yet the two men are so much together," said Nugent in an absent sort of way, as he and Gertrude advanced slowly along the carriage drive towards the house.

"I am sure," said Gertrude, rather abruptly—"I am sure you are very much hurt! You are so deadly pale. There is a seat yonder; pray, sit down and rest. Do not be afraid to lean on my arm, for I am very strong."

And Miss Usherwood led Nugent, who, giddy and faint, felt wholly unable to make any reply, slowly towards the seat.

"I am so very sorry," added Gertrude, her beautiful eyes full of tears. " I was afraid you were hurt. Just smell this eau-de-Cologne; it will refresh you." But at this moment she felt her companion's arm, which was resting on hers, slide helplessly from her, and down went Nugent on the grass, in a fainting condition

Gertrude's first impulse was to recommence the screaming process, but a moment's reflection suggested that she might do something more useful; so she bathed Nugent's forehead with eau-de-Cologne, and, undoing her basket, took out a flask of wine she had intended for Lucy Weston, and poured a little down his throat. Meantime the recumbent position, the coolness of the grass, and these remedies combined, had a good deal revived Nugent. He was able to say faintly—

"I beg your pardon, Miss Usherwood; I am sorry to frighten you so, and give you all this trouble."

Miss Usherwood, however, could not say much in reply, for she was endeavouring at that moment to bathe Nu-gent's temples, without at the same time letting her tears fall on his face, which she found rather difficult to manage. They were tears, partly arising from compassion, and partly from all the agitation she had gone through. As for compassion, Nugent had little need of any thing of the sort. It seemed to him lying there, helpless and faint, with so sweet a creature affording him aid in the gentlest, tenderest manner possible, and knowing all the time that he really had been of some service to her in the encounter with Harrill where he had received his present hurt—it seemed to him lying there, with Gertrude bathing his temples and fanning his face with her hat, which she had hastily taken off for the purpose, that he had never been so happy in the whole course of his life. He was decidedly annoyed when he felt himself getting better, especially as Gertrude no sooner perceived the deadly paleness passing away, and his eyes losing their glazed, languid expression, than she became suddenly aware of the singular appearance they must present to the uninitiated public. Therefore, placing the eau-de-Cologne within Nugent's reach, and driving away the sheep, who were now from all parts of the park approaching the spot with faces expressive of grave curiosity, Gertrude hastened homeward as fast as she could, to desire assistance to be forthwith despatched to him.

The fact was, that Nugent, in his rough encounter with Harrill, had received a severe kick on the ankle, the pain from which was so great, that, having sustained it with rigorous determination as long as he could, in the .hope of enabling Gertrude to reach home without delay, nature at length gave way, and he sank feinting to the ground in the manner described.

In a few minutes Nugent found himself lifted into a low pony-carriage of Lady Maud's, that chanced fortunately to be at the front door when Gertrude reached the house; and, despite his remonstrances, driven, not to the Manor Farm, whither he begged to be taken, but up to Beaumont-house, from which they were not now more than a couple of hundred yards distant. Here he was half carried and half supported (for the attempt to walk immediately brought back the sensation of faintness) into the entrance-hall, and placed upon a luxurious sofa. At his first appearance there was a general rush of the domestics to tender their aid; amongst them the housekeeper—bearing a bottle containing, at a low estimate, a gallon of home-made vinegar—was particularly conspicuous. Paine and the upper housemaid hovered round him, contending for the honour of presenting him with a smelling-bottle of the size of a thimble. In the background loomed two or three figures carrying jugs of water, which they seemed extremely desirous of emptying over his head; whilst the butler's voice was heard proclaiming, in accents of authority, that " The right thing for the gentleman is a wine-glass of brandy 'neat,'" Lady Maud, however, soon arrived on the scene, and the crowd immediately melted away as if by magic. She was infinitely kind and soothing, thanked him in a low voice, while she arranged the cushions for his head to rest on, for his heroic conduct in defence of her dearest child—conduct she should never cease to be grateful for; assured him that Mr. Grierson the surgeon had been sent for, that a room was preparing for him, that Mr. Usherwood and herself could not possibly allow him to leave the house, that common humanity forbade it, that the feelings of gratitude pervading the whole household would recoil from such a preposterous idea. So Nugent made up his mind to succumb, and somehow or other rather approved of the arrangement.

CHAPTER IV.

DEATH IN THE COTTAGE.

MR. USHERWOOD IS sitting over his wine in the large well-furnished dining-room of Beaumont-house. An elegant but not profuse dessert is spread on the table before him; his hands are clasped over his knees, his head is slightly bowed; he is in the attitude of one endeavouring to concentrate his thoughts upon a subject which he does not entirely comprehend.

This gentleman inherited a handsome fortune from his father, amassed in mercantile pursuits. As soon as he was his own master, Mr. Usherwood relinquished business, and devoted himself to enjoying the wealth collected by the upright industry of a whole life. He had been advised by one best qualified to advise him (his father) not to abandon business, but, if only for the sake of occupation, to adhere to it for some time longer. Mr. Usherwood could not entirely acquiesce in this view of the subject. He bought land; built a house; married a lady of rank and beauty; enjoyed the good things he owed to the labours of another; and exchanged a life of vigour and activity for one of effeminacy and self-indulgence. He grew sleek and indolent, curious in port-wine, partial to side-dishes, acquired a weakness for the most comfortable corner by the fireside; was invisible of a morning till ten o'clock; took a solemn after-dinner nap of an hour's duration, and read daily the whole of the advertisements in the *Times.* He lounged through life in his ample arm-chair, like a large oyster in its nether shell-On the present occasion Mr. Usherwood was not alone. Gertrude had quitted the room; but Lady Maud, as was her wont when there was any important matter to discuss, remained at the table, and in a low sweet voice thus addressed her husband:—

" My love, what you say contains, as it always does when you choose to exert yourself, much truth. Under ***ordinary*** circumstances I should be disposed to adhere to the *laisser* faire principle, and not precipitate, even in the gentlest manner, an affair of this nature"

"Well, now, your measures seem to me,' exclaimed Mr. Usherwood," what I call strong—decidedly strong!" " But," proceeded Lady Maud, calmly waving her small white hand to deprecate interruption, " in our present uneasy position, with the shares of the Rentworth Grand Junction Railway twenty-five per cent, below their original value, and still I fear inclined to drop"

Mr. Usherwood groaned, and helped himself to a glass of port—

" Still, I fear, inclined to drop lower and lower, I feel I must make an effort for my dear child's sake. Consider for a moment what would be our feelings if worse trials should come upon us—reduced fortune and declining years—and we should see our darling penniless and unmarried !"

" Poor dear!" said Mr. Usherwood; " poor thing— and she brought up in such luxury!"

" Our affairs, my love, are not in a pleasant state."

"I know it, Maud,—I know it now! You opened my eyes. Would I had always taken your advice! Oh! those vile, rascally railways—those man-traps for the un-wary—why did I meddle with them? "
" My dear, I am not free from blame in this matter. I had a habit of urging you to take a more active part in society and politics; and you thought to surprise me by joining the Rentworth Railway speculation, and repairing our finances whilst you won my approbation. If you had consulted me"

"Ah!" said her husband, "I was a presumptuous blockhead! If I had consulted you before I took my two hundred shares, and put my name down as a director! Yes—yes, I was tenderly led by the nose!"

"Don't fret, dear," said Lady Maud—rising up and imprinting a gentle kiss on his forehead, darkened by an uncustomary frown; "it is no use brooding over the past."

" Maud, dear, what would become of me but for you ? " he replied, pressing her hand, which she then quietly disengaged from his grasp, and, sitting down, continued her conversation.

" Our guest is a most eligible man in every respect— a gentleman, a Christian, and a descendant, as I before said, of the Tyrrells of Richard the Third's time."

"But at present destitute of much cash."

"My dear, I have reason to believe he has saved, and has invested what he has saved."

"In the Rentworth Grand Junction Railway?" asked Usherwood.

"No, my dear—a solid investment. And then, as I have before said, there is all the Clinton property actually on the brink of falling into his hands!"

"But, my dear, I must bargain for one proviso. I must, indeed!" And Mr. Usherwood resumed his concentrated attitude, and summoned a really resolute expression into his countenance. "I must not have my little girl's inclinations forced. I will not permit it. I put my absolute veto upon it."

And then, his warmth rapidly cooling as he met Lady Maud's glance, he added—" I would really prefer it should not be done, my dear;—please don't, my dear—I ask it as a favour, merely as a favour, my dear."

Lady Maud smiled graciously and replied, "Dear Richard—do you think I am going to act the haughty countess of the days of chivalry, and drag my beloved child to the altar by the hair of her head? I am con vinced she likes our friend."

"Why, she has not spoken to him half a dozen times!"

"My dear, so much the better. We are always inclined to feel most interested in those whom we see the least, but of whom we hear the most. Miss Beverley admires our guest beyond every thing; thinks him charming, noble, mysterious, and I don't know what. And she tells Gertrude all the good he does, from the drain-ing of Mashwood Moor to the establishment of adult evening schools; describes how he carried poor Hobbs, when ill of the scarlet fever, out of his cottage when the thatch had caught fire; tells how, once upon a time, he acted the village Hampden, and saved Widow Mills' garden from being thrown into a field Sir Eliot Prichard was newly fencing; tells how kindly he looks after his men, and I don't know what else; and Gertrude thinks him the *beau ideal* of the country gentleman; but then, poor dear, she has seen very few others as yet, that's true."

" But, my dear, she may admire him, but nothing more."

" I have my own opinion, my love," rejoined Lady Maud; " leave things to me. I would not, for all the wealth of California, marry her to any one against her own inclinations."

" This adventure of to-day was certainly propitious," said her husband.

" Providential, indeed!" rejoined Lady Maud gravely.
At that moment the butler entered the room hastily, and exclaimed—" If you please, my lady—if you please, sir, he's off! he's escaped !"

" What, Mr. Nugent?" asked Usherwood.

Lady Maud blushed.

" The man, sir, who insulted our young lady—the man
Harrill, my lady "

" Oh, the wretch I" cried Lady Maud. "Well, send to Colonel Clair, and ask him to order the constables to go in pursuit. I wish they could lodge him safe in jail."

"Let us have coffee, William, and I should like a small glass of maraschino, William," interrupted Mr. Usherwood. "And, William, bring me the supplement of the Times, I have not quite finished it."

They withdrew to the drawing-room, where Nugent, who had been reclining on the sofa, and partak-ing of a light dinner of chicken-broth and a wafer biscuit, was discovered, endeavouring with imperfect success to walk across the room supporting himself on two chairs.

He exclaimed, in a tone of some excitement, "I think I could ride my grey pony, if you would kindly Bend some one to the farm for him, Lady Maud!"

"Dear Mr. Nugent you must be out of your senses! You must not move an inch from that sofa till you go to bed, which ought to be—allow me to suggest—at an early hour."
" My love," she added to Mr. Usherwood, who had comfortably established himself on Nugent's sofa; " my love, you will find the arm-chair yonder a great deal more convenient for you."

Nugent, who was suffering much pain, was not sorry to resume his place, which Mr. Usherwood relinquished with convulsive alacrity. For the latter was by no means deficient in natural politeness, though a little forgetful of others when his own comfort was concerned.

"I was in hopes," said Nugent, "that I could have started in pursuit of the fellow. He cannot have got far, and, with the aid of the constable and some of my men, I am pretty sure he could have been intercepted."

" Oh, pray, never mind him—pray, never mind him ! what consequence is it ?

" cried Gertrude, who had just come in; " I only hope he will go a long way off."

"There is no doubt of that," said Nugent. "But what vexes me is Weston's extraordinary conduct. I really thought better of him!"

"Well, and what has he done?" asked Lady Maud.

"Why, I left Harrill in charge of old Andrew at the lodge, and this Weston. Harrill's arms were well pinioned with a rope. In a quarter of an hour, when the constable arrived, there was nobody to be found in the lodge but the old man tied to the leg of the table, and gagged!"

"And has Weston disappeared, too, then?"

"No, he came back just after the constable had released Andrew. The story is, that Harrill prevailed on him to go and let his wife know what had happened, as he said the shock would kill her if it was told her on a sudden. So Weston looked to see if the cord was fast round the fellow's arms, and tied another knot or two, and then starts off. Directly he is gone, Harrill slips his arms out of the cord, seizes the old man, gags him, ties him in a heap to the leg of his own table, and then makes off as fast as he can."

"Rather suspicious behaviour of this Mr. George Weston," said Lady Maud; " Paine never liked him,"

"It was very kind, at all events, to go and tell the poor sick wife," interposed Gertrude.

"Paine never liked Weston," again observed Lady Maud. "I have found out, my dear," she added to Gertrude, "that he quarrelled with the servants; and that is the reason he has not come lately for any thing for Lucy. He was shown into the servants' hall whilst Paine went for some currant jelly, and what should he do but commence arguing with the coachman, a very steady man, and a conservative both in politics and religion. The footman and some of the maids joined the controversy ; so, when Paine returned, the whole place was in an uproar, and Paine was obliged to tell Weston, civilly you know, and as it were in confidence, that he was nothing more nor less than an' Atheist.' This so affronted Weston that he left the house in a rage, and vowed he would not enter it again, unless Paine made him a written apology."

" I am not much surprised at this," said Nugent. " I rather took him by the hand when he first came; but he had a sad love for getting people about him, and speech-ifying to them on all subjects, but especially on religion and politics. I set my face against this; but he would persist, and at length established at Oxenham and other places round, what he called a ' philanthropic club,' where he gave penny lectures and spouted to his heart's content. He is clever enough, knows something about medicine, and would make a good farrier or veterinary, but love of excitement leads him on, and will not let him rest. Indeed, they do say that the members of his club vary the evening's entertainment by gambling, and have added cards to Chartism. However this may be, I have ceased to take much notice of him, and, indeed, warn my people against him."

" That's the blessing of a free country!" exclaimed Mr. Usherwood; " why, such a nuisance as this man ought to be crushed like a noxious insect! What's the use of your Boards of Health, and that sort of thing ? We want a Board of Morality. Why, a fellow like this is a walking pestilence ! Talk of removal of nuisances, indeed! Bah!" And Mr. Usherwood folded up the *Times* with a severe energy, muttering to himself, "I should like to put that sort of thing down with a strong hand, and no mistake. We want Louis Napoleon over here. So we do!"

Lady Maud now insisted that Nugent should retire to rest, and accordingly the butler and the coachman of "conservative views" were summoned, and with their assistance he was helped out of the room and upstairs to bed.

Nugent did not pass a very tranquil night. In addition to the novelty of the situation and the change of scene, his ankle became more painful; and, in order to check the tendency to inflammation, he occupied himself every now and then in applying the lotion prescribed by the surgeon—a ceremony not favourable to regular slumbers. His mind, participating in the somewhat feverish condition of his body, restlessly canvassed the events of the past day, and the curious change ot aspect exhibited by his present host and hostess, whom a few days ago he had supposed to be cold and discour-teous towards him, and whom he found now all kindness and civility. Towards morning he dropped unconsciously to sleep, and slept for an hour or two. He was awakened rather suddenly by a sustained shrill noise close to his ear, which he at first imagined was the noise of his steam-engine, combined with the lowing and bleating of all the sheep and cattle on his farm. After a minute or two it occurred to him that it must be some instrument of music in the adjoining room. It was indeed the sound of a duet on the piano, which the two girls were industriously practising. They had not played many bars, when the voice of Gertrude was heard in grave expostulation, and the music abruptly paused. The young ladies entered rather rebelliously into an argument with their sister, and the clamour of sweet voices was almost as disturbing as the " Bell Duet." Presently another voice was added to the chorus. It was Paine, who entered exclaimin.g—

" If you please, young ladies, Lady Maud desires you will not on no,account play the piano whilst Mr. Nugent is asleep next door."

Then came the addition of Miss Beverley's authoritative voice; that lady descending into the battle-field, flushed with the combined effects of sleep and wrath, and attired in a dressing-gown resembling a lady abbess's robes. "My dears, I am surprised at your want of reflection I It is really unfeeling. Mr. Nugent is seriously ill. You will certainly awake him. Shut the piano, and learn your geography." The sounds then gradually subsided, and presently all was quiet; but Nugent was effectually roused, and could no longer sleep.

In an hour or two the surgeon arrived, and looked so exceedingly cheerful over the injured ankle, that Nugent thought every thing must be most satisfactory, although he felt as if his foot was slowly roasting before a mode-rate fire.

"Well, sir, how is it?" asked Nugent.

"Why," replied the surgeon, Mr. Grierson, with a bright smile; "it's exceedingly bad. We must keep you in bed, sir, and leech you." Nugent tried to look disappointed. He said he had thought to get back to his farm that evening at latest.

"That would be imprudent," said Mr. Grierson; " scarcely judicious."

"But," asked his patient, "why so? Would there be much risk?" Mr. Grierson, bending forwards with an agreeable expression of face, as if imparting in confidence some very pleasing intelligence, answered— "Merely, sir, that I think you would probably lose your leg! We should have to operate, sir."

And, so saying, he made a rapid little flourish with his closed right hand, as if he was performing a pri
vate rehearsal of the surgical performance alluded to. Nugent had not a word more to say; and M
r, Grierson, with a joyous eye and a promise to look in that evening, quickly stepped out of the room and into the passage, where Lady Maud waylaid him, and subjected him to a strictly private interrogation as to Nugent's condition; the butler all the time accidentally standing behind the hall-door; Paine accidentally leaning her ear against the keyhole of the library door opposite; and the two young ladies boldly advancing their heads through the school-room door—an apparition which was suddenly and abruptly terminated by Miss Beverley pulling them indignantly back, and giving them three pages of French translation as an imposition.

The leeches proved so efficacious, that Nugent felt better in an hour or two, and partook of tea and dry toast on an elegant silver salver, borne by the fair hands of Paine herself, who after knocking three times at the door, and three times receiving Nugent's invitation to enter, coyly opened it, and approached the bedside with the hesitation of a skirmishing force advancing into an enemy's country

Presently afterwards came a low whispering and shuffling of feet outside the door, followed by a knock, and then Mr. Usherwood entered the room somewhat impetuously, as if dexterously impelled from behind. Recovering himself with an effort, he adopted a sickroom walk and attitude, and approached the bedside partially on his toes, with a face of mild anxiety, and making an abominable creaking with his shoes. He spoke little, and that in set sentences, as if learnt by rote the same morning. Then pressed Nugent's hand, shuddered at the dry toast and tea, and creaked out of the room

After these interruptions Nugent fell asleep, and did not wake for some hours, when he found the day drawing to a close. Outside his window he heard the musical voices of the young ladies, and, managing to get across the room, he cautiously looked through the shutters, and beheld Gertrude and her sister engaged in gathering flowers. She had a brilliant colour, for she was fresh from a long walk, and looked unusually pretty in her cottage bonnet and smart little apron with pockets in it. After gazing at her some time, Nugent fancied he heard a noise at the door, and scrambled back to bed with an air of guilty precipitation. A few minutes elapsed, and three solemn knocks were heard at the door, with a pause between each. Nugent, having three times replied "Come in!" the form of Paine became visible, and gradually invested the bed, bearing a tray on which was soup, a decanter of iced water, a second instalment of dry toast, and a tastefully arranged bouquet of flowers. Having deposited the same on a table by the bed, Paine withdrew. Nugent, we fear, did not much care for flowers; but on the present occasion he seemed to take to them more kindly, and held the nosegay in his hand for a few minutes in deep meditation. He then put them on the pillow beside him, and condescended to take some soup.

Soon the gathering gloom of twilight began to settle upon the scene around; the distant, muffled noises of a large house subsided more and more, and all was silent except the sounds of gentle merriment in the not far-off drawing-room, where Lady Maud and her daughters and Miss Beverley were sitting; sounds which spoke of a pleasant home, and social affections, and the sympathies of hearts that trust in each other, and vibrate in unison with every change and chance of daily life. Nugent's mind reverted to his own vacant and solitary dwelling, and he could not deny there was something melancholy in the contrast. His imagination roved over the farm and over the homestead and over the Manor-house itself, but shrunk back, as it were, from entering that sitting-room, once lighted up by the presence of those he loved, but now so silent, so perpetually the same; and he began to feel almost a distaste for the home of his youth, so solemn and quiet within, so busy and clamorous without. He thought that, as he sat at night in his library examining accounts, or turning over the leaves of a book, when nothing stirred except some hungry rat or enterprising mouse, and he could hear the very ticking of his watch; when, even outside the Manor-house, all was silent except the occasional faint baying of a dog, or the feeble tinkling of a sheep-bell far away, or the sighing of the wind through the leafy elms, he thought it would be well at such times to catch the sounds of pleasant voices, such as those he now heard, in some distant apartment; to know that there were kind faces, and warm hearts, and minds that felt with him and for him, somewhere not far off—somewhere under the same roof with himself.

Suddenly, however, his meditations were interrupted by a ring at the house door, and the entrance of Mr. Grierson. That gentleman pronounced him to be going on very well, and leaving some effervescing powders, enveloped in sky-blue paper, to allay any febrile tendencies, cheerfully bade him good-bye and departed for the night; was again waylaid by Lady Maud, and this time transported to the drawing-room, where he drank a cup of tea with hilarity, and talked in the most inspiriting accents. Insomuch that Mr. Usherwood woke up from his nap, imagining there was some capital joke going on; but finding Mr. Grierson was only explaining the uses and mode of preparation of a linseed poultice, relapsed once more into calm slumber.

Several days elapsed before the unexpected, yet not wholly unwelcome, guest at Beaumont-house, was so far recovered as to be able to put his foot to the ground; and, as long as this was the case, Mr. Grierson gaily but emphatically forbade his removing to his own residence. Nugent began to be a little uneasy at being thus condemned to extort hospitality from those to whom he by no means desired to be under any obligation ; yet was almost surprised to find himself soothed and gratified by Lady Maud's kind offices, and gravely asked himself whether, after all, she was not a lady of genuine kindness of heart, and great discrimination of character?

Every morning his bailiff called upon him for instructions, and reported the state of things at the farm. Next Mr. Usherwood paid him a visit of a few minutes duration, and talked invariably and exclusively of agricultural matters, having got up the subject out of the "Gardener's Chronicle" expressly for the occasion. Then the butler made his appearance with a bill of fare from the housekeeper's room, out of which he was invited to make a selection for his own private benefit. Over this bill of fare Nugent pored somewhat anxiously, a little confused by the array of French words, and not liking the idea of " Blanquette of fowl," or " Côtelettes d'agneau en papillotes," and generally ended by requesting a mutton-cutlet, plain; on which the butler invariably muttered something, that we presume was meant for "au naturel," but which sounded like " oh, natural!" and left the room as if he pitied, but made allowance for, Nugent's simplicity. Various books and newspapers were conveyed to him, and piled upon a table by his sofa. Mr. Usherwood fished out, for his recreation, an agricultural book or two from the library, about a century old, which described a newly-imported tree, termed the larch, and spoke doubtfully of the possibility of turnip culture any where but in gardens. In the evening, tea was brought to him, and every day a pretty bouquet of flowers was placed upon the tray. Soon afterwards, Miss Beverley sat down to her piano in the adjoining room, and sang one or two of her best songs, with the charitable intention of cheering his spirits; but hearing one evening from the girls (who had ascertained it from Paine), that at that precise time Mr. Nugent made a point of indulging in half an hour's slumber, she relinquished the practice, and for the rest of that particular evening was deep in "A Voice from the School-room," up-stairs in her bed-room.

It was about a week after Nugent's involuntary arrival at Beaumont-house, and the day being fine, Miss Beverley and Gertrude started for a walk. Lady Maud insisted on Gertrude's never leaving the grounds without an escort in the shape of one of the men-servants; at all events for the present, whilst the formidable Harrill was at large.

On the present occasion it fell to the lot of our respectable friend the coachman to discharge this duty, to which, as he informed the groom and footman in confidence, he made no sort of objection, seeing it was his young lady; " otherwise," he added with a portentous shake of the head, " his principles would have stood in the way of any such a thing." Coachmen, and grooms, and stable-boys, seem generally as much disinclined to walk upon two legs as if they were centaurs; and when sent on a message for a few hundred yards along the high-road, will be pretty sure to issue forth on a favourite pony, or on a valuable hunter, which of course they say needs half-an-hour's exercise at that particular juncture. The ladies then sallied forth, followed at a short distance by the coachman, whose deportment was one of gentlemanly resignation, and whose polished top-boots, as they glittered in the distance, seemed to be altogether puzzled at finding themselves scuffling along the dusty ground, instead of dangling on each side of a horse, or serenely pendant from the box-seat. After traversing several fields, and once forcing their way through a broken hedge, a feat which the coachman performed with some difficulty at the expense of a slight scratch on the nose, but without moving a muscle of his countenance, they sauntered along a pleasant green and shady lane, till they came to the main road, and presently to a gate, where Miss Beverley suddenly stopped, and exclaimed, " This is Mr. Nugent's farm, I do believe! Why, how curious we should have got here!"

" I am sure I do not know," replied Gertrude. " I only wish we were not so far from horned

"Is it not a sad pity the beautiful old house was destroyed by fire? The avenue looks so melancholy now it stands alone The old elms seem moving in perpetual procession in quest of the departed mansion."

"Why does he not rebuild it?" asked Gertrude.

"My dear—think of the thousands it would cost! I have no doubt it will be done some day, but at present I suppose it is impossible."

"Well, I am tired of standing here," said Gertrude;

" I am tired and thirsty. Could one get a drop of water at the house yonder, or was it all used to put out the fire you speak of? "

They entered the field, and reached the lawn; sending John to procure a glass of water, whilst they walked about and admired the pleasant garden and grand old trees adjacent. A prim old lady, in costume something between a quakeress and a female pew-opener, issued from the house bearing the glass of water, with the addition of wine and biscuits. Gertrude exclaimed in a low voice—

" Why, here's the great-grandmother of all the Nu-gents!"

The old lady, who was apparently Nugent's housekeeper, pressed them to come in and rest, which they accordingly did. Entering the drawing-room, they sat down on two of the thirteen chairs ranged round the table; whilst John was prevailed upon to try Squire, Nugent's home-brewed, in the housekeepers room. Whilst respectfully peeping into one of the thirteen books distributed over the table, they were startled by the sudden ringing of a bell, and presently over-heard the following conversation in the hall—

"What's your business, little boy ? What's your business ?

" Oh, please, ma'am, I want Mr. Nugent!"

It was the voice of a boy, and seemingly of a boy scarce able to speak for breathlessness.

" Squire Nugent is not here, little boy. He is on a visit to Beaumont-house."

"Oh, what shall I do?" said the boy; "it will be too late!"

" What will be too late ? " rejoined the housekeeper, rather peevishly. " What is it you want with Squire Nugent ? "

" Margaret wants him—she's dying!" was all the boy could answer.

" Oh!" answered Mrs. Finchley, " I think I know you now. You've come for soup and wine, haven't you? But, you're in such a heat, I didn't know you. And is poor Margaret going? Well, 'tis all for the best, little boy; let me tell you that."

The boy did not seem to take this consolation very kindly, but stood the picture of despondency, with his eyes fixed on the ground.

" I tell you what I'll do for you, little boy. I'll go and see Margaret myself. I will, indeed!"

And Mrs. Finchley began to tie on her head a capacious head-dress, bearing some resemblance to a bonnet.

" That won't do !" said the boy sullenly. " She don't want you."

" Well—and how do you know that, pert little boy ? " said Mrs. Finchley, shaking her head at him, and looking quite awful in the head-dress she had just donned. "How do you know that? Don't you think a poor

dying creature might be glad to see even an old woman like me? " And the head-dress waved to and fro in the dim passage, like some vast bird about to descend upon its prey.

The boy felt inclined to cry, but would not; and added—

" The parson's with her."

"Well, and that's better than nothing," answered Mrs. Finchley, somewhat more gently, for she began to discover that the boy was in great distress. "Mr. Lovell is a kind soul, I must say; though he's three parts a papist. Here—you come in, and take a cup of tea. Well, if you won't, I can't help it. But as for Squire Nugent, you ought to know, better than I do, that he can't move, because of the kicks and blows that bad man Harrill gave him."

"I was running to Beaumont-house when George Weston met me, and asked what I wanted the squire for, and said he thought the squire had gone home, and so I came back here."

The two ladies now came out of the drawing-room, and spoke kindly to the boy, who, gaining a little confidence, explained—that Margaret was near her end, and had something on her mind she wished to tell Nugent.

" I've no friend in the world but she!" said the boy, as, melted by the gentle voices and looks of the two young women, the tears rolled down his cheeks fast but silently.

"Let us go to her," said Gertrude; and, Miss Beverley at once assenting, they started for the cottage, the boy going first to show the way. At the little garden-gate in front of the cottage, a bony-looking horse, covered with foam and dust, was fastened.

" That's Mr. Grierson's horse," said Miss Beverley. The boy, after looking back, ran across the garden into the cottage, and, as he opened the door, the loud wail of several of the children burst upon the ear. Miss Beverley laid her hand on Gertrude's arm, and said, " My dear, remember! Your mother, Lady Maud, has forbidden your entering cottages without her express permission."

" That was when I was a child: I am now old enough to judge for myself;" and, so saying, the young girl opened the little gate with an energy that nearly shook it off its well-worn hinges, and hastened towards the cottage. At the door she was met by the surgeon, whose countenance was so much graver, or we should say so much less cheerful, than usual, that she scarcely recognised him.

"This is no place for you, Miss Usherwood!" he ex-claimed in a low voice. "I must beg you will not enter." Gertrude, however, followed by Miss Beverley, persisted in entering; but stopped, after taking a few steps into the room, as if awe-struck. Upon the bed lay the corpse of Margaret; her countenance pale as marble, but free from any trace of pain. Indeed, after the anxious expression the living face usually wore, its present aspect seemed mild and peaceful. A clergyman stood by the bedside, and gazed through his tears upon the even now handsome, though life-less, features of the form stretched on the bed. Struggling round, and endeavouring to reach and touch their mother's corpse, were three young children, all crying dismally. The boy Edward had caught up a fourth child, the youngest of them, and, sitting on a low stool, held him on his lap, and tried to pacify his cries.

" Oh, what will become of these little ones ? " asked Gertrude.

Mr. Lovell, the clergyman, looked with a sorrowful glance at the group round the bed, and for a moment said nothing. He was a fair-haired, good-looking young man, with clear blue eyes, and a thoughtful expression of countenance. There was something, though you scarce knew what, quaint in the fashion of his dress, which was scrupulously neat and well made.

" I have offered the lad to take him home and keep him till he could earn his bread," at length answered Lovell, "but he will not leave the little ones."

"They must all go into the house," said the surgeon, kindly but emphatically; " that is their proper place."

Gertrude not knowing what the House meant, and confused by the scene around, gave all the money she had about her to Lovell, and asked him to lay it out for them.

Miss Beverley hoped she made a "happy end."

Lovell, thanking Gertrude in a low voice for her kindness, turned to Miss Beverley, and replying to her ques-tion, said—" Pardon me, but I should wish to be excused alluding to our departed sister's last moments, except in strict confidence. I would only state this much, that I felt warranted in uttering the absolution over her, and I believe she died a sound member of our beloved church." Miss Beverley was puzzled, and set him down as a papist and a disagreeable young man.

Margaret had derived from Lovell's visits the chief consolation that had che-quered the last years of her apparently disastrous lot. She did not understand half he said, or all that he read to her; but there was something in his soothing voice, and in the sympathy shewing itself in his every look and gesture, that gave a deep meaning to all she *did* understand. And thus a gleam of religious faith rescued her, before it was too late, from total prostration and darkness of soul. She died in Lovell's arms; and though for a time distressed not to see Nugent, she yielded to Lovell's injunc-tion to commit all her cares in faith to a higher power, so that her end was more peaceful and serene than could have been anticipated by those who had seen her but a short time previously.

Gertrude and her companion now left the cottage, and found outside Mrs. Finchley and the coachman. The latter was gazing into the interior of the cottage through the little window, raising himself on tiptoe by resting his hands on the sill, and occasionally interrupting his observations in order to rub his eyes violently with the cuffs of his coat, forgetting for a time the dignity of his profession as a coachman and a conservative of moderate principles. Mrs. Finchley, adorned with her capacious bonnet, and bearing a huge basket, containing every thing apparent-ly that could possibly be needed—from baby-linen to beef-tea—looked positively tremendous; like some genie in an Arabian Night's Tale, who appears at first sight malignantly hostile, but turns out (nobody knows why) to be extravagantly benev-olent and friendly. As the ladies took their departure through the garden-gate, Mrs. Finchley bustled into the cottage, and commenced distributing buns, stockings, and religious tracts with extraordinary rapidity ; not forgetting to present Lovell and the surgeon with one or two of the latter article, selected with as much regard to their appropriateness as circumstances permitted. John, the coachman, ventured in after her, and thrust a shilling into the boy's handy with a grunt which would have expanded into a consolatory observa-tion; only he found he was in imminent danger of bursting into tears, and therefore made a rapid retreat into the garden.

"How is Lucy?" asked Gertrude of Mr. Grierson, who was just mounting his bony steed.

"Lucy? what Lucy?" answered that gentleman, fumbling in his memorandum-book. " I have five Lucys on my list—two in the house, three out. Oh! to be sure: you mean Weston?—she's better. I think she'll do. I saw her this morning, and I only wish I had as many guineas as I have ridden miles since then! This is a large Union, Miss Usherwood."

And poor Mr. Grierson was commencing his usual lament over the extent of the district committed to him, and the smallness of his salary, painting his hardships in dismal colours, but with a face of perfect contentment, when Mr. Lovell emerged from the cottage, and said—

"You will pass through Winterbourne, Grierson; will you let the relieving-officer know about this? 'Tis seven miles off, and I have no one to send.'

" Yes, yes," said Mr. Grierson; " I'll tell him. Good-morning, ladies. I must lose no more time, for I have twenty-five miles to ride before sunset." And with a deep groan, but a broad smile on his countenance, the surgeon bowed, and, spurring his steed, was soon out of sight.

Gertrude watched him disappear down the lane in a cloud of dust, and then with the governess, followed at a distance by the faithful John, directed her steps homewards in a thoughtful and saddened mood.

CHAPTER V.

SIB ELIOT PRICHARD.

THE following day Lovell called at Beaumont-house to see Nugent, and acquaint him with Margaret's decease. He found, however, that Weston had anticipated him, having brought the intelligence the evening before. He was, however, enabled to give further information, which was interesting to Nugent.

It appeared that the poor woman, fearing her husband would be sent to jail, which, drunken tyrant though he was, she could not bear the thought of, gave him notice of Nugent's intentions. The man, with many imprecations, immediately left the cottage, which he had entered soon after Nugent's departure, and betook himself to the cottage of George Weston, his intimate associate and ally. The wife, agitated and alarmed by the violence of his manner, passed some hours in great anxiety. Suddenly her cottage was entered by the parish constables and other men hunting for her husband, and informing her, in a rough thoughtless way, that he had set upon Squire Nugent and half-murdered him. This intelligence told with severe force upon the sick woman's frame. She felt she had been: the cause of her husband's -violence towards one who had always succoured and befriended her; and, though assured by her neighbours that Nugent's hurt was a mere trifle, from that hour she rapidly sank. It was her earnest wish to ask Nugent's forgiveness, as well as to speak to him on some subject near her heart The boy Edward discovered what was on her mind, and, as we have seen, started forth in search of him.

Nugent immediately sent word to his housekeeper to take care that the children wanted nothing, and place some trustworthy woman in the cottage in charge of them. His first wish was to take the boy into his service; but Lovell assured him that he quite angrily refused to be separated from the children. So, for the present, no better arrangement could be made.

Lovell was asked to stay dinner, as a few friends were expected, and Nugent had also been permitted to join the party.

Nugent could with difficulty walk, even with the aid of a good stick, so was scarcely competent to hand a lady into dinner; and it was settled, after much debate, that he should be safely seated at the dinner-table before the guests entered the room. It had rather a solemn appearance, this spectacle of a gentleman already seated; and put Gertrude in mind, though she did not say so, of the skeleton at the table of an' Egyptian feast. Nugent was introduced, with as much ceremony as circumstances allowed, to Sir Eliot Prichard, who appeared the lion of the party. With the rest of the guests, Mr. Rubbley the great mining proprietor, Colonel and Mrs. Clair, Mr. Lovell, and other residents in the neighbourhood, Nugent was well acquainted.

Sir Eliot Prichard was a gentleman who had recently succeeded to a large property in an adjoining parish to Oxenham. He was a man of large views and philosophic principles, a consistent advocate of toleration, liberal in politics, but no slave to party—at least, this was the character he wished people to attribute to him. Some, however, rebelled, and thought him shallow and bustling, a reflection of other men's theories in an imperfect and confused fashion; like a cut-glass decanter that collects a variety of lights, but all distorted and broken. Some said he was the most intolerant advocate of toleration, and the most illiberal of liberals. However this may be, Sir Eliot Prichard seemed tolerably satisfied with his own position in the world, and the opinion generally formed respecting him. His voice was soon heard at the table preponderating over others, not offensively or loudly, but decidedly, as we see a stout man of great weight push his way through a crowd without seeming to wrong any one individually, yet mildly displacing all in his way. The conversation turned naturally to the cause of Nugent's accident.

"Is the fellow caught yet ? " asked Mr. Rubbley the coal proprietor, who, with lace front to his shirt and well-oiled whiskers, looked as if he had never seen a mine in his life.

"No," said Lovell, "he is supposed to have concealed himself somewhere in your subterranean neigh-bourhood."

Mr. Rubbley did not like the mines to be mentioned in his presence, and looked hurt at even this vague allusion to them

" I wish we could unkennel him," observed Clair, who was a magistrate; "I should enjoy committing the fellow. I have little doubt he is a poacher."

" In my opinion," said Mrs. Clair, who was a lady of susceptible temper, with decided views on most subjects—" in my opinion, he ought to be hung."

" Madam," said Sir Eliot Prichard, " without taking into consideration the important question whether the individual Harrill has committed an offence which the law visits with capital punishment, I would venture to hope we shall one day see punishment by death abolished *in toto.* "

Mrs. Clair looked up at Sir Eliot as if he had said something personally insulting, and exclaimed—

" I trust, Sir Elliot, you are mistaken I *I* like our good old English customs too much,,to hope any such thing!"

" We must look at this question in its broadest bearings," continued Sir Eliot—pausing in the act of carving the haunch of venison, much to the distress of Mr. Usherwood, who was waiting in an agony to be helped— and glancing round at the company in general. "What is the object of death punishment ? Clearly, the benefit of the survivors. Now, look at that horrid spectacle, the cold-blooded execution of a human being—Mr. Usher-wood, I believe you are partial to fat—a human being like ourselves—the same limbs, thews, sinews—a little more gravy, Mr. Usherwood ?—the same feelings, fears, and hopes—and the same *soul,* Mr. Lovell"—he added, dropping his voice to a solemn whisper as he glanced towards the clergyman—" and the same soul as we have. What a scene of vice, rioting, and intemperance! "

" I can't help that," said Clair, gallantly taking up the cudgels for his wife; " Government ought to put all that down. It is very hard that a murderer should be let off because a lot of rascals as bad as himself choose to misbehave at his execution. Government ought to put it down."

"Put it down, sir!" continued Sir Eliot. "This is a free country; we don't want one of your paternal Austrian governments over here. No, no, my good sir, you can't make men virtuous by Act of Parliament; can you, Mr. Lovell?" he added, turning to the young clergyman.

Lovell answered, that he thought capital punishment wiped out the stain of blood from the land, and was commanded by Holy Scripture.

" Excuse me," said Sir Eliot, drinking a glass of champagne, and pausing to appreciate the flavour. " Much reflection has decided me to totally discard the antiquated interpretation of the passages to which, I presume, you refer."

Lovell, not wishing to drag the Scriptures upon the table any further, was silent; but Nugent maintained that a careful examination of Scripture, conducted in proper spirit, would lead any conscientious man to believe that death punishment was recognized and sanctioned by divine authority. Sir Eliot, impatiently waving his hand, proceeded:—"A public execution is a barbarous, offensive, and appalling disgrace to modern civilization. Talk of gladiators, the inquisition, bullfights, and such-like horrors, indeed !I'll trouble you, Colonel Clair, for a bit of the breast.—By the bye, Colonel, have you ever seen a man hanged ? I have. Thought it a public duty. Paid ten guineas for a front seat in the garret window of a pawnbroker's shop. A horrid sight! We took our prog with us, of course: champagne, veal pie, and cigars. And I do assure you, Lady Maud, I cannot describe the inhuman callousness of the crowd that filled the space beneath our windows. I saw two fellows drinking gin and water, and smoking clay pipes a-top of a lamp-post right in front of the gallows. There was a pickpocket as busy as a bee in one direction, and in another I counted no less than three men with black eyes; whilst many of the mob were so drunk that only the excessive crush kept them upright on their legs."

"All this is very sad," said Lovell; "but, after all, these painful sights are not proofs of the ill effects of death punishment, but symptoms of the vices deep-seated in human society."

" To be sure, Mr. Lovell," now joined Mr Usherwood, who was considerably taken aback at Sir Eliot's views. " To be sure—that' it! Just like measles or scarlet fever. Never mind the eruption; that's a healthy effort. Go to the root of the evil, and try and cure that."

"Well, I'm for private executions, at all events"— observed Nugent.

" 'Twould be such a sneaking, hugger-mugger aflair," said Mr. Usherwood; "much like an inquisition. Doesn't look British, that sort of thing. Now, I hate every thing that is not honest, downright British. William! Fill my glass with that light French wine I'm partial to. Thank you, William."

"Nobody can deny," urged Nugent, "that executions are an opportunity for in-dulging in most disgusting excesses; and I think, too, that coarse minds are only brutalized by the spectacle of human suffer-ing."

"Who would believe the culprit was really dead?" asked Mr. Bubbley, with a shrewd self-satisfied glance round the table;" who would believe it ? You'd have a jury, would you I A jury to witness the execution? Nice task for a jury! Fancy be-ing impanelled to stare at a man being put to death in cold blood! Nice morning's amusement!"—(with another shrewd smile)— "Pleasant, humanizing, edifying oc-cupation!"

" Well, but you provide that amusement, that occupation for thousands, as ex-ecutions are now conducted," suggested Nugent.

"Thousands, sir!" exclaimed Mr. Rubbley, Warmly. " Why, who really sees an execution out of all the thousands present! It's only a few near the scaffold, The rest only see figures like puppets mov-ing to and fro a long way off. That don't hurt any body."

"But, if that is so," said Gertrude timidly, "it must be as difficult to prove that a man is really dead in public as in private executions. Only a few actually see the ceremony in-either case."

Gertrude's remark did not seem to be heard by Mr. Rubbley, but Nugent ex-claimed—

"Thank you, Miss Usherwood, I think that disposes of Mr. Rubbley's argument. To my mind, a mob is a very indifferent witness to a matter of fact."

Just then Lady Maud asked Sir Eliot how the poor creature looked when led out to be hung ?

"My lady," rejoined Sir Eliot, "I couldn't detect the expression of his counte-nance very distinctly, although my opera-glass was a good one. But I can only tell you this; the whole thing looked uncommonly like a murder."

"Why," said Colonel Clair, "the poor creature had slain his own wife, and made mince-meat of her corpse in order to dispose of it conveniently!"

"I should like to have seen him minced alive!" observed Mrs. Clair, crushing up her beef *rissole* in the agitation of the moment.

" That's a narrow view of the matter," responded Sir Eliot. " This unhappy man was once young, innocent, playful—perhaps engaging. Nay, I don't hesitate to say he was once a baby—his mother's cherished darling. Ah! Lady Maud, Mrs. Clair, Mrs. Rubbley, you are mothers— consider! Doubtless, once upon a time Greenacre and Rush trundled their hoops in childish glee, and Mrs. Manning nursed a doll!"

"Well, but what would you do with these fellows? Am I to have my throat cut?" expostulated Mr. Usher-wood, settling his shirt-collar with a soothing forefinger.

" Such men as these should be put in a reformatory," replied Sir Eliot—" a national reformatory."

"We should need a precious large building!" inter-rupted Mr. Rubbley, with an attempt at sarcasm.

"A reformatory establishment, with an efficient staff of carefully selected officers, whose hearts are in their work, male and female—Lady Maud, male and female. Apart-ments airy and cheerful. No extraordinary luxuries, but every necessary comfort. Moderate recreation, occasional solitude, lectures, sacred music, useful and moral publications; Mr. Lovell, clergymen of every denomination. In short, a graduated course of spiritual and physical education, issuing, as soon as the patients should be pronounced convalescent, in a cer-tificate of moral health; first, second, or third class, according to the quantum of merit fairly attribut-able to each of them. Oh, it's an interesting subject— very!" '

And Sir Eliot paused to drink the pale ale handed to him after cheese.

"Thank you!" exclaimed Mr. Usherwood; "thank you. I'm sick of reformatories! There was one near our last place of residence, and it did precious little good. 'Twas a reformatory for boys; and, would you believe it, twenty per cent, of these boys turned out badly? Twenty per cent., instead of becoming virtuous young Christians, ran wild, and played the deuce I"

"I beg you pardon," asked Lovell; " but how many Eton and Winchester lads are virtuous young Christians, do you think, sir?"

" Oh,that's quite a different thing, Mr.Lovell !" replied Mr. Usherwood.

"It does gall me," said Lovell, `` to see lads often or twelve, sons of labouring men, marched off like felons to the county jail for a month's hard labour, just for robbing an orchard or pulling a turnip, when we know very well a young gentleman detected at these tricks would only get a birching, or may be fifty lines of Homer to write out'

" We generally flog lads for that if the case come within the act," remarked Clair. "I'm a hearty advocate for flogging."

"The worst of it is," said Lovell, "that some boys suffer so much, and some so little, from punishments of this kind. You cannot regulate the degree of punishment you inflict."

" Thrash them till they halloo loud enough!" said Mr. Bubbley with a knowing look.

" Then you punish a boy for being plucky and bearing pain well, and reward him for effeminacy—or, what is worse, for hypocrisy; for any one can shout or yell."

"A friend of mine," said Lady Maud, "a young married friend of mine, with some nice children growing up, adopts the practice of pricking them with a pin when naughty. She considers that it answers well."

"What a beast!" murmured Lovell quietly to his -next neighbour.

" A dose of physic and early to bed is my plan!" said Mrs. Clair, in an emphatic voice.

"Ah! but they make a fuss over physic," remarked Mrs. Bubbley, "and it tries my nerves; I cannot bear a fass."

"Bad—very bad!" oracularly observed Sir Eliot. " The solitary system is *the* method of punishment. An enlightened parent should adopt no other. Let the culprit ruminate in utter seclusion, and regulate-the amount of light allowed to him in exact proportion to the enormity of the fault committed. The ladies should see our county jail—should they not, Clair! Keep the body cramped, cooped-up, confined: then let the mind work, work, work—that's the way to reform a culprit!"

"It seems to me," said Lovell, "we generally think too much of punishment, and too little of reward. If you give a fair share of encouragement to those in your charge, the withdrawal of it will be a punishment severely felt. We ought to sweeten the atmosphere of life in some of its phases. A little kindness and sympathy would not be thrown away even in jaila or workhouses."

" What! kindness to *criminals* ?" asked Rubbley, opening his eyes very wide. " To *criminals* ? "

" I would never deprive a man of hope," rejoined Lovell. "I would allow even a criminal to better his condition in some degree, however trifling, by his own exertions. Then, as for the community in general, I would offer apprenticeships and other advantages to the children of the working-classes; making it a condition that they should regularly attend school for a certain time previous to the examination they would have to pass, and allowing so many marks for good conduct, and so many marks for proficiency in study."

Sir Eliot, who did not like to be merely a listener, and thought Lovell was trespassing on his peculiar province, now rather abruptly turned the conversation to the subject of spirit-rapping; at the same time observing to Lady Maud, in an under voice, that the young man was "well-meaning but prosy."

Soon after, the ladies withdrew, much to Nugent's regret. He was just beginning to feel quite at ease with Gertrude, with whom he had been for some time conversing, and had actually succeeded in interesting her in topics which he at first feared would put her too much in mind of the school-room; such as the instinct of animals, and the different species of wild-flowers in the neighbourhood.

Gertrude on that occasion was indeed easily pleased, for it was her first dinner-party, and, quiet and ordinary though it was, it had the charm of an unusual excitement. . What a change from early dinners and schoolroom discipline!—from Miss Beverley's "My dear, you're sitting quite crooked !"—and Lady Maud's " My darling child, don't take any more of that jam-roll; it's as heavy as lead!" And Agatha's and Jessie's vociferous petitions, " Gertrude,. Gertrude, you never give us enough gravy,—I wish you would let Miss Beverley carve!"

Now, all around her were full of the most anxious politeness, and somehow or other the gentle respect showing itself in Nugent's tone of voice, and in the expression of his eyes, pleased her more than she would have liked to confess. It was so new to feel that there was one sitting by her who seemed ready, at the slightest signal, to do any thing whatever she chose to command.

When the men were left alone they became more argumentative, and Mr. Usherwood fell asleep. Clair, Mr. Rubbley, and Nugent, discussed free-trade and protection, but found that each of the three differed entirely from the other two; so that they kept revolving round one another, like planetary orbs with centrifugal energy, ever approaching but never coalescing. Lovell was entangled for a short time in an argument with Sir Eliot on the Athanasian creed; but both, on a sudden, finding themselves out of their depth, paused to collect their thoughts; which enabled Sir Eliot to overhear the triple controversy waged by the three other gentlemen at the other end of the table.

" **Rain** to the agricultural interest, which has been the bulwark of Britain for !"exclaimed Clair.

" Salvation to the country at large, imperilled by class legislation!" interposed Rubbley, who was picking his teeth with an elegant gold toothpick.

" Some compensation seems but just, considering vested interests. Local burdens should be reduced," urged Nugent.

" A feather in the balance—mere sham!" cried Clair

" What, tax the poor to replenish the pockets of the rich? " asked Rubbley.

"Rents mnstfallforatime,at all events/' added Nugent.

" Robbery!" shouted Clair.

" Panic !" exclaimed Rubbley, and then followed a medley of words, in which high prices—low prices-native industry—alarming abundance of bread—monopoly —Manchester—' wages —paupers —peers—Peel-were chiefly distinguishable; and in the midst of which Sir Eliot descended upon the combatants with the' grandeur of an avalanche crashing down the side of a mountain upon three goats fighting at the bottom. He fell heavily upon all three. Rubbley was stunned. Nugent endured the shock with passive resignation. Clair writhed in involuntary prostration. Sir Eliot had got through half a page of John Stewart Mill, only interrupted by a faint snore from- Mr. Usher-wood, which the speaker mistook for a smothered sigh of admiration, when the butler entered the room with coffee, and the party broke up and joined the ladies. Nugent was tired, and glad to escape to his bed-room, leaning on John's shoulder. As they ascended the stairs a melancholy ballad issued from the school-room, which John evidently thought highly of, for he stopped unbidden to enable Nugent to listen. That gentleman, however, we regret to say, propelled the coachman forward, and did not avail himself of the musical treat offered to him.

The fact was, that Miss Beverley, who on this occasion had been specially in- vited to join Gertrude's first dinner-party, had met with a trying slight. The footman had omitted to hand her currant jelly when she was helped to hare. 'Tis true she could not endure currant jelly, but that the footman did not know, and therefore she felt the omission as a studied affront. So she had fled to her school-room, and was consoling herself by singing "None remember thee!" in heart-rending accents. This assertion, however, sang several times by Miss Beverley, with her eyes fixed on the picture of a favourite lap-dog hanging on the wall opposite, was practically refuted by the entrance of Gertrude, who came to fetch her back to the company.

Nugent overheard animated whispers and conversation, and finally laughter, after which Miss Beverley followed Gertrude back to the drawing-room, where she was, not long after, again engaged in singing "None remember thee," in much the same affecting accents as before, but with a lighter heart. Mrs. Clair praised her performance in a patronizing way, and was prevailed on by Lady Maud to sing a duet with Gertrude; but as Gertrude was imperfectly acquainted with the words, and Mrs. Clair had forgotten the accompaniment, the attempt was only partially successful, and ended in a compromise that they should sing in succession their own songs.

Gertrude had rarely sung even before such a moderate assemblage as the present, but got on very well; only Mr. Lovell **would** turn over the leaves too soon, and that with such a solemn expression of face that she feared to remonstrate; and Miss Beverley would sit just before the piano, exhibiting an agonized anxiety for her pupil's success in a variety of ways; beating time with her tea-spoon on the saucer; smiling wildly when asked by Sir Eliot Prichard what was the name of the song; frowning authoritatively at Gertrude when her voice trembled a little as it dwelt on G Flat. Insomuch that Lady Maud at length gently led her to the other end of the room to play chess with Colonel Clair, who had never played before in his life, but, fascinated by Lady Maud's winning manners, assented to her proposal without a moment's consideration. Accordingly, the colonel passed the remainder of the evening in the agreeable occupation of learning the moves; a task so distracting to his brain, that he dreamed, after retiring to rest, he was a knight at chess, vainly striving to move in the oblique fashion peculiar to that piece.

Mr. Rubbley talked about railways to Mr. Usher-wood, whom he endeavoured to inspire with those sanguine views which, "after mature deliberation," he himself had embraced. A task not very easy, seeing that Mr. Rubbley was in quite a different position to Mr. Usher-wood, having purchased a large number of shares in the stock of the Rentworth Railway Company with his own iron, and sold them again before the great fall took place. Barring this slight difference in their relative circumstances, they got on very well; and Mr. Usherwood, until cooler reflection dissolved the hallucination, felt comforted and refreshed, and even went through the form of confidentially drinking " Prosperity to the Rent-worth Railway!" in a glass of negus, aside to Rubbley. Rubbley, though he knew it was a mockery, re-echoed the sentiment in a jovial whisper.

Sir Eliot complimented Lady Maud on Gertrude's appearance with the air of a man of large experience in feminine beauty and accomplishments; and asked many questions, circuitously and diplomatically, about the same young lady: the answers to which Miss Beverley with her quick eye observed him secretly enter in a small memorandum-book, whilst pretending to admire the portrait of Lady Maud's late lamented great-grand-mother, "the countess of Del afield."

CHAPTER VI.

THE RIVALS.

IN a day or two Nugent was once more reinstated at . the Manor-house Farm, and immersed in business both in-doors and out, for work had of course fallen in arrears during his enforced confinement to a sick-room. The change from pleasant society in a large luxurious mansion, to his own solitary and secluded home, was great; but Nugent felt it was his duty to resist any tendency to discontent or weak depression of spirits, and did his best accordingly. During the day his many avocations, involving, for the most part, active personal exertion, rendered the task comparatively easy; but,with the darkness and stillness of night, the trial became more severe. Once or twice, indeed, during the first week following his return, he had recourse, by way of transient consolation, to a talk with Mrs. Finchley; but that lady's topics were invariably of a complexion rather dismal. She descanted on the misfortunes and sufferings of the Nugent family—described the illness of his late father— gave the fullest account of his mothers funeral—narrated the death-bed scenes of personal friends in the neighbourhood—quoted several sentences out of "Dre-lincourt on Death," and all this in so unearthly a tone of voice, like the ghost in Hamlet, that his spirits sank lower and lower, until he made an effort and rushed out of the apartment. Even then his trouble was not over; for, in the course of the evening, Mrs. Finchley, anxious on account of his health, followed him into his study, bearing a glass of some nauseous mixture from the family medicine chest, which she almost forced down his throat; but, finding he could not be prevailed on to swallow it, drank it off herself, lest it should be wasted.

He did not wish to show any importunity in renewing his intimacy with the Usherwoods; but Lady Maud was careful it should not drop. Notes and messages— inquiries after his health, and invitations to dinner— were frequent; and at length Mr. Usherwood and Lady Maud paid a joint visit to inquire about a lady's horse Nugent had heard of, and which he had recommended for Miss Usherwood's use. In the course of conversation, Nugent, on the impulse of the moment, offered to take charge of the animal for a few days or weeks if necessary, and break him thoroughly in, lest he should prove too fiery and headstrong. This proposal, which was grate- fully accepted, led to Nugent's riding with this young lady once or twice a-week, accompanied by one of the younger girls, as well as the faithful John. Now and then they took a gallop along the downs above the Manor Farm. Both were fond of this particular ride, and gave their horses the reins without speaking, hut in silent en- joyment of the free and rapid rush over the elastic turf and through the fresh moun- tain air. John and the younger sister followed at a sedater pace; the one apparently in a state of solemn reverie, the latter impatient at the restraint imposed on her.

It may be said that these attentions on the part of Nugent were decidedly marked and unmistakeable; but it must be remembered that he was some ten years older than Gertrude—a difference at her age of some importance. Moreover, the parents of the young lady encouraged his joining her for the sake of the advantages accruing from his instructions in the equestrian art.

Nugent, indeed, deluded himself into the idea that he looked upon her merely as a child—a sort of younger sister; but in a little time found her image begin to haunt him in a way unfavourable to agricultural interests: found that at times his heart beat very fast, and his breathing suddenly grew oppressed—symptoms en- tirely new to him, and always exactly coincident with a rencontre with Miss Ush- erwood, whether it was at a dinner party in the neighbourhood when she glided in after Lady Maud; whether it was during a solitary ride when he saw far off, on the crest of the hill, or turning the corner of some shady lane, a lady on horseback, whose light and buoyant figure he re-cognised with half a glance. Although prone to examine his thoughts and feelings, it must be confessed that on this occasion Nugent did so with reluctance, and after some delay. As often happens, he postponed to make an inquiry, the result of which might possibly prove painful. Accustomed to obey his conscience, he postponed for a while putting his conscience in possession of the facts requisite for forming a judgment. This, however, was a weakness in which Nugent was too honest long to indulge. He was haunted by doubts, whether he was such an one as Lady Maud would deem qualified in rank or fortune to be the husband of her favourite child. Again, he recoiled from the idea of taking advantage of the opportunities confidingly granted to him, or of a young girl's inexperience of the world, and of her acquaintance only with the scanty society of the neighbourhood, to win her heart or her hand.

About the time, however, that Nugent began seriously to question the prudence and the blamelessness of his familiar intercourse with Gertrude, a circumstance occurred which induced him to make up his mind more rapidly than he probably intended. He had promised to meet Gertrude at a particular bridge that spanned one of the many streamlets traversing the valley, in order to take one of their usual rides. At a few minutes after the appointed time, Nugent slowly rode up to the bridge in question, and to his surprise, but not exactly to his gratification, observed, besides Gertrude, her sisters, and the coachman, another person—a gentleman well mounted, who seemed in animated conversation with Gertrude. On approaching the group, he found this addition to their riding party was no less a personage than Sir Eliot Prichard, quite at his ease, and in high force.

Nugent, vexed at having kept Gertrude waiting, exculpated himself by producing his large hunting-watch, a legacy of his father's, and declared that the rest of the party were ten minutes before the time of rendezvous.

Sir Eliot, who greeted Nugent with an air of good-humoured toleration more annoying than any degree of stiffness or hauteur, instantly produced an elegant Geneva watch, and assured Nugent that his timepiece must be out of order, for it was at least a quarter of an hour slow—an assertion which the chimes of a church clock, not far distant, at that moment chanced to corroborate. The fact was, that Nugent's methodical habits and attention to punctuality had been of late rather relaxed, and his watch, usually kept in accurate order, had suffered in consequence. He instantly owned his fault, but this trifling incident gave him some annoyance. They all forthwith started for their ride. Sir Eliot invited himself to be of the party, and coolly, as Nugent thought, took up his position at Gertrude's right hand, leaving him, the lane being narrow, to trot behind, sometimes with one of the girls, sometimes jostling against John. Now, John having been enjoined by Gertrude to keep exactly ten yards behind her sisters, rigidly adhered to the order, and sternly pressed forwards despite every transient interruption, whether it was a score of bewildered sheep, springing to and fro in every direction—whether it was an agitated regiment of ducklings floundering in the middle of the road, having temporarily lost their presence of mind—whether it was a corpulent cart horse escaped from a field and accidentally entangled in the procession of riders, trotting onwards with a calm and satisfied eye, as if he thought he was no small addition to the respectability of the party.

As soon as they got into a broader road, Nugent left the two young ladies to John's care, and rode forwards until he was in a line with Gertrude and her companion. For some time he had not an opportunity of putting in a word. Sir Eliot was fluent, and, not being oppressed with modesty, brought readily to the surface of his mind all that a retentive memory had stored there. Gertrude seemed decidedly amused. Then when Nugent did say something in explanation of a local legend or superstition, Sir Eliot waited when he had done speaking as if he expected more to follow; politely bending his ear towards him in patient anticipation of the point of the story. Having thus mildly damped Nugent's inclination to talk, Sir Eliot began to ask questions about his farm, his crops, and his live stock, as if adjusting his conversation to Nugent's farmer-like calibre.

"By the bye, Mr. Nugent," he exclaimed, pointing with his whip, " that's your arable yonder, if I mistake not. You'*ve got it into very fair order now. It must be hard work for you walking over that clay land. But I suppose you arm yourself with stout shoes, and a good honest pair of gaiters. How are oats now? Flattish, I fear. Ah 1 you must have many an anxious night of it. Yes, Miss Usherwood, you may smile, but farmers have a wearing life of it; a wearing life. Up early and down late! By the bye, Mr. Nugent, I should like to buy a likely young sow, if you can spare one. You are famous for pigs, I know. But then you don't spare trouble with them, I'll be bound. Why, there's Wriggles now, a tenant of mine. He gets up at two in the morning to turn his prize pigs over on their side with his own hands, and feeds them with suet dumplings! How do you like Gubbins, the new landlord of the ' Jolly Farmers?' I believe that's where you put up on market-days. Much company there! Ah! I'll answer for it, you have many a merry meeting after the cares of the market! Gubbins was my groom, and is a good judge of malt liquor; at least he ought to be, for he has swallowed a good many hogsheads in his day. Don't you let him impose on any of you, Mr. Nugent. He's a sharp dog."

In this strain Sir Eliot persevered, seemingly intent on exhibiting Nugent in the light of a commonplace yeoman. Now, Nugent never pretended to be any thing else than he really was, and at first took Sir Eliot's allusions quietly enough, thus frustrating the attempts of his companion to make him ridiculous in Gertrude's eyes. His gentlemanly ease provoked Sir Eliot, and goaded him on farther than he meant, so that Nugent began to comprehend his drift, and seek-ing to give Sir Eliot a check exclaimed—

"I don't know much about the ' Jolly Farmers,' Sir Eliot; but certainly some of my fraternity patronize it, and from what they tell me, I suspect Mr. Gubbins, your late groom, to be rather a mischievous' fellow. They say he amuses his customers with no end of anecdotes about his late master."

"What, with me, sir? with me, sir!" replied Sir Eliot, suddenly scarlet with indignation; then commanding himself, added—" Ha, ha, ha! a droll dog—a droll dog!"

" He has a story about the late election, in which you were defeated."

"Aha! has he?—a droll dog, very! Miss Usherwood, wouldn't you like a gallop on that nice bit of turf? "

"Oh! I should so like to hear about the election," exclaimed Gertrude, provokingly reining in her horse.

" Do tell us, Mr, Nugent! It's only fair to Sir Eliot."

"Ha, ha, ha!" exclaimed Sir Eliot; "it's a good story; I'll tell it myself. My people shut a blue voter up in a clock-case at the town-clerk's office—he was tipsy of course, and snored so loud that every one thought the clock was bewitched, and the beadle was sent to fetch the parson! Now, shall we gallop ? "

"I don't mean that, Sir Eliot; it's another story," said Nugent. " I mean about the green-grocer's children suffering from hooping-cough, who had a violent fit of hooping as your opponent passed the window. You thought they were yelling out denunciations against him, and. kissed them heartily all round! Do you remember?"

"Come, come, come! shall we gallop?" asked Sir Eliot, impatiently spurring his horse forwards.

We fear that Gertrude rather enjoyed this indirect contention between her two companions. There are few women who dislike being the occasion of a little jealous rivalry and animosity. Not only the novelty of it pleased her, but all the feminine instincts of a girl of eighteen were at work in her breast.

Accordingly, as they neared home, and Sir Eliot was about to take leave at the corner of the road leading to Winterbourne, Gertrude exclaimed— " Oh, I have had a delightful ride! I am sorry it is over.

" Perhaps," said Sir Eliot, " you will allow me the pleasure of joining you in some of your rides ?"

"I don't make fixed appointments," said Gertrude, laughingly. " If any knight-errant overtakes me in my excursions, I permit him to form one of my suite, provided I feel sociably inclined, and like his colours and coat-of-arms."

"And whither then, fair princess, and on what day will your steed next bear your peerless form ? "

" Oh! that I do not know. Perhaps this day week, at the same spot and the same hour as to-day, but I make no promises."

Sir Eliot waved his hat, put his hand to his breast with a devoted air, and galloped off. Nugent felt his heart sink. He was grieved and angry, chiefly, as he was fain to believe, because of his brotherly interest in Gertrude, and because he regretted to witness any exhibition of levity towards such a man; but really, we suspect, because he did not like another to be placed on a par with himself, and that other Sir Eliot Prichard.

No sooner, however, was Sir Eliot gone, than Gertrude turned to him with a malicious smile, and said, "And you—oh knight of the rueful countenance!— will you venture in quest of me this day week ? "

Nugent gravely begged to be excused, and taking leave, with an air as he thought of tranquil dignity, but really of profound vexation, rode slowly homewards.

Gertrude brandished her little whip, and with cheeks dimpled with smiles, and eyes sparkling with enjoyment, cantered away towards home.

Nugent, we are sorry to say, returned to his dusky library, anxious, dispirited, and vexed. His friendship with Gertrude seemed to fade away like a thin cloud that traverses the face of the moon—a moment bright, the next lost in the midnight sky. That he should have excited in the mind of a young and fascinating girl a kindly feeling and a certain degree of interest, had been a source of hope and comfort to him. That she should invite to her side a man, who in her presence had almost in-sulted him—a man who, whatever his talents, possessed a vulgar heart, and whose words and works plainly showed that self was his all-sufficing idol—argued a low moral taste on her part and a want of consideration for his feelings towards her, which seemed at once to open a gulf between them not easily to be crossed. As for coquetry, or feminine playfulness, Nugent did not know much about matters of this kind. He was simple and straightforward; and it is probable would not have been made much happier if a friend had suggested that Gertrude simply wanted to make him jealous.

On his return home that day, he found amongst his letters that had just arrived, one from Sir Lawrence Clinton, acknowledging in a friendly manner the letter of condolence he wrote to him some four or five weeks since, which Sir Lawrence said his distressed state of mind had prevented his doing before. The old man wrote in a more cheerful tone than might have been expected. He informed Nugent that his London physician thought it probable that a mild climate would check the disease from which his son was suffering, and all agreed that the experiment was at least worth trying.

His father, therefore, intended immediately starting with him for the south. Nugent sat down and wrote a few lines of a hopeful character, offering to be of any assistance which the confusion of a hurried departure might render acceptable.

Then leaving the writing-table, and throwing himself into a rather uncomfort-able arm-chair with a very short upright back—the easy-chair, *par excellence,* in the room, he gave way to some half-hour's meditation. After which he rose, took down a book entitled ' Comfort for the Afflicted " from the shelf, and read it until the daylight began to fail. Even then, however, he still sat before it, with eyes fixed vaguely upon the now illegible page, and one hand supporting his brow. He was interrupted in his reverie by the entrance of Mrs. Finchley with candles, followed by the country girl who performed various offices in the establishment, bearing a tea-tray. The housekeeper still kept up some kind of state, and, unless the maid was engaged in incongruous occupations, never brought in her master's meals without being attended by her.

"Finchley," said Nugent, "have you found any good woman yet who will take charge of the Harrill children!"

"No, Squire Nugent. I have trudged all over the manor—your manor as was once—and the ungrateful folk make no end of difficulties about it. Widow Maddocks would take one; Mrs. Jenkins, another; and old mother Wrench would take the third; but then, you see, she has got the rheumatics sadly, and they do say she drinks; and so I fear she wouldn't do justice by them. As for Mrs. Maddocks, she's a good, quiet soul enough, and works hard, and is as honest as you or me, sir, but then she's no Christian."

" And Mrs. Jenkins ! " asked Nugent.

" I'm disappointed in that Mrs. Jenkins; she talks, but that's all. I thought her a decent woman, and fond of a tract; but I have a misgiving what she likes best is your broth and skim-milk, Squire Nugent. She'll only take one child, and wants too much for that."

" Well, we must wait a while; we may hear of something by and bye."

Mrs. Finchley snuffed out the candles twice, in her agitation, at the very name of Mrs. Jenkins. For only the day before she had met that worthy returning from the village shop with half a pound of butter wrapped up in the identical tract she had begged Mrs. Finchley to give her that very morning, with tears in her eyes. Recovering herself, however, with an effort, Mrs. Finchley smoothed down her ancient silk dress, and, courtesying solemnly at the door, took her departure.

It may be well to mention here, that the village of Okenham was unexpectedly relieved of Harrill's motherless children. Some well-to-do relatives of

Margaret's, in S—shire, volunteered to take charge of them. Edward, however, who was regarded as an illegitimate son of Harrill, was not included in the offer; and, whilst Nugent and Lovell were debating what to do with the lad, Harrill himself managed to get hold of him, and carried him off to one of the coal-mines at Reniworth.

Some days passed, and Nugent was once more seemingly absorbed in farming occupations. His men noticed the renewed interest and activity he exhibited, and discussed this change of demeanour after work was done—round the blacksmith's shop, on the churchyard stile, over their firesides, or at the beer-shop—with that intense earnestness with which labourers discuss the most trivial incident relating to their employer.

He received more than one invitation from Beaumont-house; was honoured with another visit from , Mr. Usherwood; was presented with a pine-apple of mountainous dimensions, the gift of Lady Maud. The invitations he politely declined; the visit he eluded on the plea of business; the pine-apple he accepted, and presented it to Lovell; from whom it passed to the school-children, who were all under the care of Mr. Grierson the surgeon, on the following day. Thus, Nugent's intimacy with the family at Beaumont-house came suddenly to an end. To all appearances he was much the same as previous to his visit there, with the exception of a few eccentricities noticed by Mrs. Finch-ley; such as a strange indifference to her choicest dishes. This she attributed to a taste corrupted by the delicacies of Beaumont-house; whilst Lovell observed that he came to church on Sundays a quarter of an hour before the service began.

Sir Eliot Prichard had ridden with Gertrude once, at all events, since their last meeting: how often besides he did not know. On the occasion referred to, Nugent chanced to be overtaken by the riding party, just as he was accompanying his bailiff into a field through which there was a bridle-road. He was in everyday costume, and possibly Sir Eliot really did not recognize him; but that gentleman cried out in a tone of authority—" Hal-loo ! one of you—just open that gate for us !" Nugent thought he heard Gertrude call him by name, but he only turned round, and, gravely raising his hat to the advancing party, desired Maddocks to open the gate, whilst he himself crossed the road, and struck into a piece of arable on the opposite side. Nor did he stop un-til he had traversed two or three hundred yards, trampling down the ripe wheat with unusual recklessness, and causing unspeakable anguish of mind to three young trespassers in the act of devouring unripe blackberries at an adjacent hedge, who concluded he was in full pursuit of them.

Sir Eliot, who had no intention of seriously affronting Nugent, but simply la-boured under the notion that in love-making and courtship all stratagems were lawful, left his card upon him the next day through the agency of a small groom, clad in neat livery, astride of a very large horse. This young gentleman handed the card with difficulty to Mrs. Finchley; having to stoop down so far that he almost threw himself, as well as the card, into that lady's outstretched hand. Then, in an easy way, requesting a light for his cigar, to the disgust of Mrs. Finchley who pre-tended not to hear him, and bowing gracefully to Nugent, whom he saw at the win-dow, he trotted off, and disappeared from sight some time before the large animal that bore him. This apologetic move on the part of Sir Eliot was duly acknowledged by Nugent, who sent his card to Winterbourne —Sir Eliot's seat—by the hand of the gardener's boy, tidily wrapped up in a piece of old newspaper.

Whatever may have been, however, Nugent's secret intentions, and however deliberately he may have laid down a plan for his future guidance, an occurrence took place which he either had not foreseen, or had not sufficiently taken into ac-count, and completely baffled his calculations.

He did not often approach the park surrounding Beaumont-house. One day, however, having been calling on Colonel Clair, whose house was situate on the side of the valley opposite to his own, he felt an inclination to choose for his way home a pleasant lane passing by a picturesque little church, about a mile and a half from Beaumont-house. It was the same lane we have already briefly noticed. Nugent had two or three times ridden in that direction in company with Gertrude. As he approached the large walnut-trees rising at intervals over the grass sward which clothed the hill-side, his countenance became sadder, and, stopping for a few min-utes, he thoughtfully surveyed the scene. A little distance from the lane, near a lofty walnut, whose straggling branches, heavy with fragrant leaves, cast a cool shade on the ground beneath, Nugent suddenly detected, half-concealed in the grass, a lady's glove. He took it up, and hastily searched for some name or mark by which to identify it. The initials, " G. U." written in the inside, met his eye.

Nugent stood for a moment without moving. A struggle seemed to be passing within him. Then, as if acting under some stern impulse, he dropped the glove where he had found it, and abruptly turned to depart On turning round, however, he perceived, seated at the foot of one of the trees adjacent, a young lady with a sketch-book on her lap, on which she had been drawing, But her eyes were now turned towards Nugent, and her hand no longer held the pencil.

It was Gertrude. The meeting was embarrassing to both parties. Nugent would have bowed and passed on; but she regarded him so calmly and sadly, with an expression so different to what he had last seen on her countenance—not making the slightest advance towards him, but sitting in grave contemplation of his movements—that his resolution gave way, and coming towards her he said, in a confused sort of way, that he hoped she had been quite well since they had last met. Looking down, she replied in a low voice—

" I should never have spoken to you, Mr. Nugent, as long as I lived, if you had not first spoken to me."

"I beg your pardon if I have been rude—if I have in any way offended you."

" You may have been rude; but it does not follow I should have thought it necessary to be offended," answered Gertrude a little proudly.

" I would suffer much—indeed I would—rather than give you the smallest cause of annoyance," continued Nugent. "I have felt severely the cessation of all intercourse between us. Some of the happiest hours of my life have been spent in your society. But why do I revert to them ? They are past—they are gone by for ever! I have striven, Miss Usherwood—I have striven hard to forget you"

" Thank you," interrupted Gertrude, with something like a smile. " That was friendly."

" I have striven to forget you," continued Nugent; "to devote myself to worldly realities; to walk in the light of common day; but the task is hard."

" Pray," exclaimed Gertrude, " what is the meaning of this excitement—of this animosity towards me ? What is all this mystery about? If you have taken a dislike to mamma, and to all of us—say no more about it, but avoid us for the future. None of us will thwart you in your determination."

Gertrude quietly took up her pencil, and began to draw, but her hand slightly trembled. Nugent stood before her, endeavouring to weigh his words. Then he said—

" Miss Usherwood, believe me, there are few living creatures towards whom I bear animosity; towards you least of all. I have not intruded on you of late for many reasons. I believe a secluded life safer and better for such as I am."

" Well, if that be so, far be it from me to argue the point. Perhaps, however, you will condescend to give me my glove, which I think I saw you fling away just now."

Nugent coloured and picked up the glove, without, however, returning it to Gertrude. He then said—

" Forgive me, but I cannot explain all that passed through my mind when I saw and touched this glove. I know that I am slow and awkward—a mere farmer, as your friend considers me and treats me—"

" Whom do you mean by ' my friend ?'" asked Gertrude, with anger flashing from her eyes, and a heightened colour.

Nugent, in a rather faltering voice, answered—" I mean Sir Eliot Prichard, who so often accompanies you in your rides, and who almost insulted me in your pre* sence."

" How unkind—how unjust I" exclaimed Gertrude, rising suddenly, and speaking with rapidity. " It is very wrong, sir—it is very unseemly to call any one my Mend. I am surprised you should treat me so"

Nugent stood in some confusion. In a moment she would be gone, and yet she looked so very lovely, even in her displeasure. So with precipitation he exclaimed—

"I heartily and sincerely beg your pardon! Indeed I am very sorry. Do not leave me thus!"

Gertrude hesitated, and Nugent taking courage, said—

" Let me keep this glove merely as a token of forgiveness. Will you, Miss Usherwood ? "

His voice betrayed more feeling than he wished; but Gertrude, sitting down on the low rustic bench from which she had risen, said—

" No! It would quite upset all your plans about for-' getting me."

" Do not leave me without a kind word," pursued Nugent. " I know we must part; of course so *i* but do not let your last glance be scornful and indignant"

" Why do you provoke me, then ? " replied Gertrude. " What right have you to taunt me about any one I choose to ride with ? "

" Forgive me—I have been insolent, presuming!" exclaimed Nugent earnestly.

"It was kind, most kind of you to suffer me to accompany you at all. It was not my place to interfere with you, or dictate to you what friendships you should form. Say that you have forgiven me. I shall return to my solitary home with a less heavy heart if you will say that you forgive me, and that we part friends." Gertrude's head was turned away. Aftera pause she said, half to herself whilst she hastily collected her drawing materials—

" To think that I care for that disagreeable man! I cannot bear him! I wish I had never seen him I"

She rose abruptly. Nugent was disturbed by the conflicting thoughts that rushed through his mind. A* haze seemed to spread over the landscape round him. He felt, however, that she was going from him, and that he should never perhaps have an opportunity of speaking to her again. In a voice indistinct from emotion, he almost involuntarily exclaimed "Gertrude!" She turned her face suddenly, and he saw that it was bathed in tears. The next instant he was seated beside her, pressing her hand to his lips, and uttering, as the gravest men are apt to do under the circumstances, a great many extravagant things.

Meantime, the butler at Beaumont-house was waiting to sound the gong for dinner; but Miss Usherwood was not forthcoming. Gradually the whole establishment was in commotion at her non-appearance. A party of light infantry, consisting of two footmen, all the gardeners, and a page who had once been shapely, but now presented a decidedly bloated aspect—aided by the cavalry of the garrison, consisting of the coachman and groom—scoured the vicinity of the mansion. Lady Maud walked up and down the lawn in front of the house in some uneasiness. Mr. Usherwood followed her example, keeping about ten paces distance, and diversifying the promenade by an occasional retreat to the entrance-hall, where he refreshed himself with sherry and water. The two girls sat in a corner of the school-room conversing in whispers, and, carried away by the general excitement, sometimes shed tears, and sometimes kissed each other. Miss Beverley gradually worked herself up to a pitch of desperation, and seizing a nightcap she had been furtively trimming, put it on her head in mistake for a bonnet; rushed out of the house by a back-door;

and hurried along the highroad without the least idea where she was going, but under a full persuasion that she was materially assisting in the search for Gertrude. The screams of mingled admiration and amusement which her peculiar head-dress elicited from some school-children in the road re-called her to herself, and she stopped, with professional promptitude, to rebuke their rudeness. Discovering the next instant the state of her toilette, she abandoned the field precipitately, and fled homewards indignant but abashed. As she reached the house, she found that the missing Gertrude was safe at home, having just returned through the shrubberies at the back of the house.

It was not particularly agreeable to Gertrude's feelings to find such an extraordinary bustle and excitement pre-vailing on her account. It seemed as though her recent interview with Nugent had been specially noted, and witnessed by every member of the household, and was somehow intimately connected with the disturbance. She blushed to the tips of her fingers as Lady Maud and her father alternately took her in their arms, and caressed and scolded her in one and the same breath.

"Naughty child!" cried Lady Maud. "How you have heated yourself! Kiss me, darling. I am quite angry with you."

" Poor thing—poor thing!" exclaimed Mr. Usherwood, pressing her to his side, and smoothing her long hair from her foreheads " How her heart beats! Why, you must have run all the way home! Have a glass of sherry, dear; there's some in the hall."

" Sherry, my dear!" interposed Lady Maud. " How can you talk so? Lean on my arm, dear, and let us go in. Here, Paine," she added, as that domestic appeared at the hall-door with the never-failing diminutive smelling-bottle in her hand, " shut the windows in my room; there is too much air there."

" Shut the windows in Lady Maud's room!" re-echoed Mr. Usherwood in an energetic voice. The two sister* now emerged from the school-room in a state of uproarious rapture. Miss Beverley, what with sympathy, fatigue, and excitement, sat down on a flower-stand to the serious discomposure of a row of Jenny Lind ge-raniums, and energetically wiped her eyes with the head-dress before alluded to, crumpled up into a small muslin ball, from whence depended two long strings of white tape. Gertrude, who by this time was beginning to laugh and cry simultane-ously, was hurried off by her mother, and, at her own earnest request, left alone. The various parties sent to explore the neighbourhood dropped in one after anoth-er, hot, jaded, and dusty. John the coachman appeared last, having made a formal circuit of the estate, in compliance with Lady Maud's injunction. Presently after, old Andrew crept up from the lodge, carrying his venerable gun, and inquiring if he could be of any use. Soon the house was restored to peace, and Lady Maud and Mr. Usherwood sat down to dine off burnt soup, fish boiled to jelly, and fowls partially reduced to ashes, with much relish and satisfaction.

CHAPTER VII.

NUGENT IN THE CONFESSIONAL.

NUGENT returned home in rather an exhilarated state of mind. Certainly it was very delightful to find that so sweet a girl as Gertrude Usherwood cared for him in the smallest degree. His heart beat lightly as he strode homewards. Objects he had seen that very morning bore now a different aspect. That piece of grass was not half so brown as he had thought it to be. The swedes were coming up pretty well, after all. That ploughman yonder had really ploughed the furrows not so very crooked. He was sorry he had chided him so sharply about it. He would give him a bit of tobacco next time he passed him at work. The Manor-house looked quite pretty. Many people would admire it, he thought. Then, the fine trees, and the rich landscape all round, with the far-off roar of the sea the other side of the hill; it was not so bad, after all! The library is dark; but how soothing in the glare of a summer's day! A great deal might be made of that house, he thought. The drawing-room, and some of the bed-rooms, must be new furnished of course; and then the room with the mullioned-window, looking into the lawn at the west end, would make quite a lady's boudoir. He was buoyed up with a strange, new feeling of joy. His eyes would

now and then grow moist with tears, he scarce knew why. Thoughts more vivid
and varied than usual traversed his mind. He sent Maddocks home grinning from
ear to ear at some humorous saying, and astonished Mrs. Finchley by a hearty shake
of the hand on entering the house. Soon, however, graver con-siderations presented
themselves. He was a conscientious man, and had not felt this unwonted access of
good spirits very long, before he began asking himself—" Have I any right to be so
happy? Let me see—let me reflect." He began to feel less satisfied as the first glow
past off, and the sober realities of to-day's history were calmly unfolded before his
mind.

It was true that Gertrude Usherwood had looked upon him kindly, gently, even
tenderly, that very day. It was true that he had felt her small hand tremble with
emotion as he held it in his own under the shade of that old walnut-tree. It was true
that those lustrous, dark-coloured eyes had for a moment looked up at his face with
a kind of shy, tremulous, self-reproachful glance of affection. It was true that that
musical voice had dropped lower and lower as it half confessed the sympathy and
love which its very softness and hesitation had already revealed. This was true. Yet,
who was Gertrude? A young girl, barely eighteen, brought up in luxury, accustomed
to every species of refined enjoyment, reared in the expectation of largely sharing
in the gaieties and distractions of fashionable life; little acquainted with any but
those of her own sex; little acquainted with the real predilections and antipathies
of her own heart. Even if her parents consented to their union—which Nugent in
his modesty much doubted, and, had it not been for the civilities recently lavished
upon him, would have thought preposterous—could she herself, could Gertrude, be
happy in a quiet secluded home, with a man indeed devoted to her, but of different
tastes to herself, not familiar with fashionable life, and obliged by the nature of his
avocations to be much and often from home ?

These thoughts cast a shadow over his mind; but in such questions the judgment is often disturbed, and the heart dethrones the intellect. We endeavour to
give due weight to the painful suggestions of experience and of conscience. We
pause and ponder—' but the next moment a throng of pleasant fancies come rushing through the brain; plausible ideas spring into life on all sides; the shadows fade

away; hope stimu-lates our whole being; the present is a whirl of enjoyment; the future lies bright and warm in peaceful sunshine.

Had Nugent been gradually informed of Gertrude's partiality towards him, he would doubtless have retained more complete command over his feelings; but he had been wholly taken by surprise. His very humility and diffidence had been a snare to him. It had not occurred to him that any one woman, much more one whom he regarded as a sort of lovely vision in quite another sphere to his own, could exhibit real, positive affection for him. It was strange and thrilling to feel that such a being was ready to go with him wherever he would, and share all his fortunes with a loving confidence.

He could not all at once tear her image from his heart, and trample under foot these sweet anticipations of happiness. He owed something, he thought, to herself. He had, without any selfish motive, or rather quite unconsciously, made an impression on her heart and in a manner linked it to his own. It would not now be right abruptly to sever himself from her, unless indeed her parents distinctly and formally urged him so to do. They must decide for her, and by their decision he would honestly abide.

Nugent lay awake most of that night, musing over what had occurred, and almost against his will picturing to himself the scenes the future might have in store for him. Sleep, however, came at last, and he did not awake until the farm-yard and offices in the rear of the Manor-house began to re-echo with the customary clamour of each returning day, softened indeed by distance, and by intervening shrubberies and trees; but still, to the attentive ear, plainly and continuously audible. Then as Nugent hastily arose, in the light of a grey autumnal dawn, feeling still fatigued with the unwonted excitement of the day before, the great event on his memory rose distinctly before him, no longer softened and adorned by the touches of an exalted fancy, and the glow of a heart unaccustomed to the gentle agitation of love. He felt inclined to despond : to rebuke himself severely: to cast about for some means whereby he might undo what had past. It was not for himself he feared, but for Gertrude. She may have been surprised into an affection for one who would never suit her as a husband; who would never have attracted her if she had been previously introduced into a larger sphere of society.

After having transacted some of the usual business of the day, Nugent sat down to breakfast; but the home-made rolls were scarcely touched, the new laid eggs, the delicate slices of broiled ham, the fresh water-cresses, were pushed aside untasted.

" I really think this is a case for consulting some one," he said.

For the reader may understand that Nugent was not a man generally inclined to run after people for advice. The notion, then, of consulting any body, betokened that he was seriously agitated.

"But whom?" There was no one in the vicinity who, for one moment, seemed to him a fit recipient of ' his confidence save Lovell. As his clergyman, Lovell it might be supposed would have been the natural resource for his troubled mind, and the first person to occur to him. But, unhappily, the difference in their views and in their tastes kept them more apart than was good for either. Not but that to a certain degree they liked and esteemed each other; not but that they wished well to each other, and hoped the best for each other. Still, considering that Nugent had been brought up by Puritan parents: had read little in theology but the works of those divines of the English Church who fraternize most with Puritans: had seen a good deal, not merely in Lovell's principles, but in his practice, which gave him pain and vexation: it was not likely he should take warmly to him as a friend and companion, or derive from his ministrations, and from his near vicinity, that comfort and assistance which every clergyman ought certainly to afford to those over whom he is appointed pastor.

It may be said that there is a distrust, a reserve, a self-sufficiency on the part of the laity, which necessarily repels the ministers of religion, and ties their hands. It may, however, be questioned whether there are not a number of minds amongst all classes, who would not feel great comfort and relief in sometimes engaging in intimate converse with their clergymen, provided those clergymen gave them due encouragement so to do. But such encouragement cannot be afforded by any abrupt or formal demonstration. It must be tendered in the shape of earnest sympathy and unselfish anxiety, not once or twice a-year, but whenever occasion offep. It must be apparent in the general tone of the clergyman's bearing, both inside and outside the house of God. Moreover, it is desirable that some knowledge of human nature, not merely of patristic human nature, nor of collegiate human nature, but of Eng-lish human nature—without reference to class, sta-tion, or employment—should have been acquired by any one to whom a cure of souls is committed.

Returning to Lovell, then, he was a really devoted land single-hearted parish priest. It might be said that his whole heart and mind were in his work. The church bell rang regularly for daily prayer. The village school children saw him daily at the self-same hour, and listened to his premeditated instructions. The sick and suffering knew his face quite as well as their doctor's; his purse was open to them, more than was perhaps strictly prudent; his earnest prayers and tender sympathy reached their hearts better than any amount of material gifts could have done.

Such plain tokens of sincerity and zeal could not but win the esteem, not merely of the poor, but of the sturdy farmers in the parish, who to speak without ceremony like to see their clergyman fairly earn his stipend. Nevertheless, Lovell had some enemies in the parish, and very few hearty friends except amongst the labouring class. He was often at issue with half his congre-gation ; was suspected to be a Pa-pist; had from time to time thrown the whole parish into a state of hot water; had seriously disturbed the equanimity of that useful referee, the " oldest inhabitant." With the best intentions, with a devoted heart, with an amiable disposition, he of-ten created an alarming tempest, and that about the most trifling points. This partly arose from want of general information, and too limited an acquaintance with the habits and feelings of ordinary English-men;—partly from following too implic-itly the dicta of literary men, contributors to magazines in vogue amongst his own set or amongst clergymen whom he justly admired for *some* good qualities, and therefore conceived must possess *all* good qualities. Thus, he would adopt a crude theory, or seize a sudden notion dropped from the brain of one of the leaders of his theological school; theories and notions filtered through the discolouring medium of many minds before reaching his own. He would take up some idea of this sort, and with a vigour, in itself creditable, endeavour to cany it out in defiance of every difficulty, and shutting his eyes to all immediate consequences. It was unfortunate that Lovell had no men of his own way of thinking to advise with, of maturer judgment and more enlarged experience than himself. There was indeed Smithers, late Fellow of Oriel, who had been prevailed on to accept a pleasant living some miles from Oken-ham. Smithers was a man of vivacity and parts, but had grown grey in the discharge of onerous collegiate duties—the enjoyment, that is to say, of literary leisure, architectural tours, select wine parties, and small tea-meetings where the air was redolent of eau-de-Cologne and popery. Smithers had all his own way at Sweet-borough. It was a snug little parish, with rectorial and vicarial tithes thrown together, and a great squire who was for a wonder liberal with his purse. The two or three principal ratepayers were the squire's tenants, and they passed their leisure hours in admiring the squire, and the squire's parson, namely, the Rev. Augustine Smithers. Therefore, Smithers did exactly what he liked. But he forgot that all his brother clergymen were not so fortunately placed. Still he was decidedly looked up to by the high church clergy, and his opinion regarded as law. There was Smithers then to advise him. As for the bishop of the diocese, Lovell had heard that there was one, but was not yet personally cognizant of the fact.

Now, the first thing Lovell did on entering upon his ministerial duties, was to make some reforms in the performance of divine service, and in the internal arrangements and fittings of the sacred edifice. His predecessor had been a good quiet sort of a man, with inadequate notions of his responsibilities. People were rather glad to get a more active man. His predecessor read the communion-service from the reading-desk. Lovell very properly restored the practice of reading the service in front of the Lord's table, within the precincts of the chancel But, not content with this, he went to some expense in erecting a carved stained-deal screen, to separate the chancel from the rest of the church, which sadly obstructed the free passage of his voice. It was reverently meant, but the farmers were first puzzled and then angry. They could not hear him; so he was obliged to thrust his head right up against the screen, in order to make his voice audible. Again his predecessor used, when the first lesson was long, or had several proper names in it, to substitute another in its place. Lovell of course dropped this indecorous practice, but took care to introduce the bidding-prayer before the sermon. This he repeated in a rapid monotonous tone, which made half his congregation stand aghast. It was soon currently reported, that Lovell used Latin prayers during divine service.

Smithers one day took him by the button, and assured him it was the correct thing to preach after the third collect at evening prayer, and not at the end of the service. Lovell, accordingly, did so, but the congregation supposed he had merely taken the liberty to omit half the prayers, and accordingly they quitted the church directly his sermon was over, without waiting for the conclusion of the service. So he thought the plan did not entirely answer, and discontinued it. Then he had a grand dispute with Nugent about the royal arms. They used to hang above the commandment tables. Lovell said they had no business in the church at all. That it was erastianism—dangerous subserviency to the civil power—in fact, sheer idolatry. The other churchwarden having been in a state of imbecility for some years, and only retained in office from regard to the feelings of his family—the whole battle was between Nugent and the young clergyman. Nugent said he was no courtier, but it was his duty to see that no disrespect was done to the Queen, the first magistrate in the land. It ended in a compromise. The royal arms were removed from the east end of the church, and hung up at the west end. They were newly painted for the occasion, and the lion and unicorn came out with a ghastly splendour, which sent a thrill of loyal awe into the hearts of the school children.

Lovell, however, with Nugent's cautious co-operation, did some real good in the church in the way of repara-tion and improvement, but created a frightful disturbance, by restoring the nose and three fingers of a small stone figure under a sculptured canopy in some out-of-the-way nook of the building. Nobody had ever quarrelled with the figure before, and never would have done so, but when they saw the renovated nose, and the restored fingers, there was a great outcry; and one old lady (related to the imbecile churchwarden) wrote a long letter to the archbishop of Canterbury on the subject. The archbishop blandly interfered, and it ended in the nose and fingers being removed. After which the storm was appeased, and Lovell and the statue submitted to their disappointment with becoming fortitude.

Nevertheless, Nugent, when in real trouble or anxiety, knew no one in the vicinity whom he could consider a fitter person to consult than Lovell; partly because Nu-gent felt he was thoroughly in earnest, partly because he was so full of sympathy with the distress of others. Con-sequently, after a little consideration, Nugent set out for the parsonage, which was at no great distance from the farm. As he crossed the road, which descended the hill behind the farm on which the par-sonage was situ-ated, he saw in the distance a figure coming in the same direction as himself. It was clad in white voluminous garments, and Nugent could not tell what to make of it. On coming closer, however, he perceived that it was no other than Lovell dressed in his surplice with an ordinary hat on his head, endeavouring as he moved along to prevent his dress from sweeping the ground by holding it up with one hand. Perceiving that Nugent was a little perplexed at his costume, Lovell, after exchanging a few words, observed in an explana-tory tone of voice—

"You see, Mr. Nugent, I have lately come to the conclusion that the clergy ought to go to and from the church in their ministerial vestments. We sadly undervalue in modern days the utility of external appearances. A clergyman in his surplice passing through the village is a signal that the church is about to open for public prayer, or that public prayer is just concluded. I have just been saying matins."

Nugent thought the surplice had rather an eccentric look, particularly in con-junction with the hat.

" Why, you see," Said Lovely " there *was* an unpleasant sensation created; and Smithers recommended I should make Some concession. Accordingly, I laid aside the college cap which I wore at first with my surplice, and adopted a plain 19th century hat. I hope this compromise will be received in the spirit it is offered. But here we are at the parsonage! Will you come in, Mr. Nugent ? "

Nugent followed the young clergyman into his house, a mixture of farm-house and cottage, with a little flower garden in front) and a little kitchen garden behind that might have been productive, had it not been for the depredations committed by poultry, pigs, and dogs, from neighbouring cottages and farm yards. Those individuals paid him periodical visits both by day and night, and slightly disturbed the equanimity of Lovell's gardener, a lame old man, whose principal horticultural exertions consisted in waging war upon the trespassers above mentioned. The sitting-room was simply furnished, but contained a handsome book-case, pretty well stocked with standard works, and a few good prints hanging against the walls. There was also a fine old Elizabethan arm-chair, into which Nugent was about to throw himself, but was gently stopped by Lovell, who intimated that it was too worm-eaten and crazy to bear any one's weight. Selecting then a more substantial seat, Nugent, whilst his companion divested himself of his surplice, proceeded to state, in a voice of much composure but with a heightened colour, that he had something on his mind about which he desired to ask Lovell's advice. The young clergyman, who, having attired himself in a dressing-gown of great length and composed of black cloth, looked awfully monastic shut the door of the sitting-toom, and, proceeding to another part of the room, threw open a small door leading into a sort of boudoir, or oratory, the furniture of which ap peared to consist of one high-backed chair and a large hassock.

" If it is any thing very serious," said Lovell, " perhaps we had best step in here."

" Oh, not at all—at least, this room will do just as well!" replied Nugent, rather disconcerted. " The fact is, you see it is a matter in which a young lady is concerned—a young lady in the immediate neighbourhood —a person to whom I am very much attached—and I wanted to talk the matter over with you, feeling doubtful what course to pursue. You see marriage is a serious step, Lovell, both for her and me."

" Oh I" was Lovell's rejoinder, and with that he reclosed the little door he had just opened, and with a countenance exhibiting a slight shade of disappointment, tempered by amusement, he sat down opposite to Nugent, and waited patiently for the latter to open his mind more fully.

It was some time before that reserved nature unwound itself completely, and enabled Lovell to comprehend the rights of the case, and the causes of his uneasiness. Lovell's first impulse was to adjourn the interview, and confer with the Rev. Augustine Smithers, late of Oriel, in the mean time. But there was no room for delay, and Lovell was thrown upon his own unaided resources. He took Nugent's hand with a sudden friendliness and said —" I tell you what, my dear fellow, I don't see what you can do but go to the young lady's parents, and put yourself entirely in their hands. Of course, I have a pretty clear notion who the young lady is, and all about it; and I must say, my private impression is that the parents approve of the match, and, in fact, have purposely thrown you together. This being so, they are quite as responsible for what may happen as you yourself are. I should say, go at once and talk the thing well over with the parents. Give them all due authority in the matter; for as Miss Usherwood—I beg a thousand pardons—I mean the person to whom you are attached, is so very young, they should certainly be the arbiters, and decide for or against a marriage."

" But I fear," said Nugent, " I fear we are not suited *to* each other! I fear there is too much discrepancy of tastes not to say inequality of age!"

" Excuse me," said Lovell, " but you ought to have thought of that before."

" True enough," rejoined Nugent; " but you see I never thought she would care for me. However, I will take your advice, and put myself in her parents' hands;" and he rose to depart.

"By the bye," interrupted Lovell, "how came it you were not at the vestry meeting yesterday? "

" Why, to tell the truth," said Nugent, " I was afraid I should be forced to take part against you, and so, as yon had plenty of adversaries without me, I stayed away."

" I had, indeed," rejoined Lovell. " There was a sad exhibition of insubordinate, not to say unchristian feel-ing!"

" Your proposal was to do away with some of the pews, was it not T " asked Nugent.

"With all ! I wished to destroy them all! I wish I could sweep them from the face of the earth. They are blots and ulcers on the fair face of our beloved mother the Church."

" Well, and how did you get on ?"

"Oh! I concisely explained how offensive and unsightly those huge deal boxes without lids, must be in the eyes of ' every man of enlightened judgment, enlarged religious sympathies, and correct architectural taste.' I thought this rather neat, but it made no impression beyond eliciting a laugh from your brother churchwarden, who, notwithstanding his imbecile condition, was brought into the vestry for form's sake. Then I urged upon the rate-payers the impropriety of thrusting Christ's poor into the worst places in the church, where they bitterly felt the cold and could scarce hear their clergyman's voice—still no impression ! Whilst to my profound disgust, I fancied I heard some one snoring close behind me! Then I explained how the pews took up a great deal too much space, how they screened the ill-behaved from observation, how they obstructed sound and promoted damp; in short, I thought my arguments happily conceived and forcibly put, but saw only a host of blank immovable faces all round me as stolid as Madame Tussaud's wax-work figures, whilst nothing was heard but the occasional insane laugh of the churchwarden, and the steady snoring of the farmer behind me. At last I touched upon the sin of making distinctions between rich and poor, and advocated complete equality in the house of prayer. Immediately the whole place was alive. There was positively almost a row. Every body found a voice. I had fairly excited them at last. Farmer Gorse shouted out that there ought—' ought,' he said with a thump on the table— there *ought* to be a difference between rich and poor in church. That I wished to turn the world upside down. That my opinions were ' clean contrairy to human nature.' Farmer Walrush turned livid with indignation, and swore he never hadn't stood, and he never wouldn't stand radicalism, chartism, sixpenny points, or any such-like sociable tricks! As for Mr. Salter, the thin, smooth-tongued grocer, he leant across the table and began to prove the Scriptural propriety of pews by the text in St. Matthew's gospel, directing us to ' go into our closets when we pray, and shut the door,' winding up by .the quotation, 'The poor, shall never cease out of the land.' On which Farmer Gorse cried 'Hear, hear,' till he was nearly choked! As if that had any thing to do with it! Another farmer scratched his head and said, ' If the pews went, he knew his missus would make him go to meeting;' an intimation which was greeted with quite a cheer. Is it not deeply distressing? Is not this ignorance, this moral obliquity, almost appalling? Now don't you think so, Mr. Churchwarden ? Come, now! " and Lovell put his hand appealingly on Nugent's shoulder.

"You tried for too much," said Nugent; "I don't particularly like those large pews, and think the poor are somewhat hardly used; but I don't like free seats; they are so uncomfortable, not to say Popish."

" Why, the members of the Roman communion," replied Lovell, "have no free seats. They usually hire chairs for the occasion. Fixed benches are Anglican, but not Roman."

" Well," said Nugent, " I like to be sore of my place."

" Smithers says," observed Lovell, " that at Sweet-borough they have no inconvenience whatever. The congregation, generally upwards of thirty, all know their seats and there is no confusion at all"

" I tell you what," exclaimed Nugent, " I do not mind your lowering the sides of my old family pew"—this he said with the air of having made up his mind to a great sacrifice. "In feet, to show you I really do not like pews, I don't mind if you remove it altogether I It is not the original family pew, because that, you know, my fether pulled down thinking it too grand for a man who was earning his bread, and I don't mind if you raze it to the ground. 'Tis certainly too high and bulky, and takes up half the chancel archway. But mind, Lovell, you must put me a door to my open bench,"

"I will—I will!" cried Lovell, much elated, "and then there's the strangers' pew!
"

"Pull that down, and fix some open seats for the old people, the poor and sickly;
there will be room for twenty, at least, if you manage well."

The strangers' pew was a huge square enclosure, opposite to Nugent's pew,
occupying considerable space. It was intended for occasional visitors to the parish;
but, as visitors were rare, it was usually invaded and occupied by all the idle young
men and women in the neighbourhood, who, beneath the shadow of its wooden
walls, eat nuts, carved their names on the seats, and wrote love-letters to one another. Lovell accepted the offer with joy, and, rushing to his bookcase, began to
hunt for sketches of poppy heads, panels, and mouldings for Nugent to choose from.
That gentleman, however, felt his thoughts wandering elsewhere, and begged to
take leave.

" I am glad I may smash the strangers' pew!" exclaimed Lovell,. as he escorted
Nugent to the door. "By the bye," he added, leaning over the gate, after Nugent had
got some distance down the road, "Do you know the correct way of spelling 'pew?'
It should be p—u—e! Doesn't it sound contemptible? p—u—e! You will find it all
explained and proved in the second number of the ' Mullion Magazine,' p— u—e!"
This he uttered with a most scornful emphasis and in a raised voice in order that
Nugent might hear him. Then, withdrawing his body from the gate, returned into
the Rectory.

Nugent pursued his way homewards; and, having ordered his bay mare to be
brought round in half an hour, retired to his room and dressed himself with unusual
care; and soon after mounting his horse, he galloped lightly over the turf in the direction of Beaumont-house.

CHAPTER VIII.

THE YEOMANRY AT RENTWORTH.

No sooner, however, had Nugent reached the further extremity of the field, and, passing through a gateway, found himself in the main road, than he began to slacken the bay mare's speed until she dropped into a walk.

His line of policy was not so clearly defined as to render him very impatient for the interview with Lady Maud. The animal he rode soon began to evince unmistakeable sympathy with her master's deliberative mood. Occa sionally she would halt in the middle of the road, occa- sionally diverge to one side, and browse calmly on the leafy hedge, not without turning back an inquiring ear as if to ascertain what Nugent thought of it. When her master shook the loose reins with admonitory impatience, she would step out with cheerful alacrity, as if it was what she was just wishing to do, but would again begin to stray and saunter along the road as soon as Nugent relapsed once more into a musing reverie.

The bay mare had just thrust her head oyer a gate into a field, and was endeav- ouring to make acquaintance with a spindle-legged colt performing various idiotic capers a few yards off, when the sound of a horse galloping towards them at full speed along the road, roused both Nugent and his horse from their respective trains of thought.

The next moment a man, booted and spurred, approached at a gallop, but di- minished his pace as he came near; finally pulling up short as soon as he was face to face with Nugent. He held out a packet of letters to Nugent, at the same time exclaiming—

"The yeomanry are called out, sir! There are riots on the Rentworth Grand Junction. The navvies have torn up the rails, and half killed the superintendent and the clerk of the works. The police seized the ringleaders, and carried them prisoners to the inn at Rentworth; but the navvies have been joined by a body of miners, and the town is in danger of being attacked. Colonel Plover hopes you'll get your troop together in time to meet him at Rentworth by sunset. He has had some trouble with the farmers because it's harvest time, but they are coming together at last."

Nugent instantly turned his horse homewards, but at a steady pace, for there was plenty of work for the animal between that time and sunset. He read his written instructions as he wént along, occasionally questioning the messenger who accompanied him.

Without going minutely into the causes and nature of the present outbreak, we must explain that, for some weeks past, great discontent had prevailed amongst the navigators and labourers along the Rentworth Grand Junction Line, in consequence of the company having reduced their rates of payment both by day-work and by the piece, and shown increasing irregular rity in the customary weekly advances of cash to the contractors for the works on their line, and to the labourers immediately in their employ. Then again there were ugly rumours afloat of the critical position of the company. The shares dropped weekly, and the very efforts made to curtail expenses only augmented the general uneasiness and suspicion. The last dividend declared had been at the rate of 4 per cent., but it was paid! as the initiated well knew, in great measure out of capital, and not out of the receipts on the completed portion of the line. A committee had been appointed at the meeting of the shareholders to audit the accounts of the company, and thoroughly investigate the proceedings of the directors. That committee sat daily, and daily broke up with black looks, and ill-suppressed indignation. All this added to the impatience and excitement prevailing amongst the gangs of labourers along the unfinished portion of the line. Provisions were dear, and a strike in some neighbouring coal-pits, which had lasted some weeks, let loose upon society a number of men, full of bitterness of spirit and ripe for mischief. At this juncture came the great smash and exposure of the Rentworth Railway. It was discovered through the haze intentionally flung over its affairs, that the company was at present plainly and undeniably insolvent. One or two directors absconded to Boulogne. A secretary bolted to America, having previously left his hat and stick by the bank of a river, to make the public suppose he had drowned himself. Several subordinate employes thought this a bright idea, and did the same things so that for two or'three days you perpetually found reposing on the brink of the river, hats rather the worse for wear, whose owners had vanished from the scene.

It was Thursday when the worst was known, and the men working on the line were paid on a Friday. The committee of shareholders of which the directors were *ex-officio* members, decided on appealing, as they termed it, to the good sense of the labourers, and paying them a respectable percentage on wages due, that is to say, two-and-sixpence each, with the promise of more next week. The result plight have been anticipated; the sub-secretary, deputed to address the men, was received with shouts of execration. A navvy, more impetuous than his comrades, seized a lump of coal from a heap near the station, and flung it at his head. It was the signal for a general outbreak.

The railway terminus at Rentworth was attacked by a mob of about two hundred men, women, and boys. The cash-box, fortunately not heavily laden, was seized, the contents scattered in all directions, and snatched up by the strongest or most active. Much the same scene took place at two or three other stations, where the men were in the habit of receiving their money. The better disposed were carried away in the stream. One station-house was partly burn,t and partly torn down,

After the station-house was destroyed, and the mob for the most part scattered, two or three policemen and a body of special constables arrived on the scene, and, with some difficulty, succeeded in capturing two of the most obnoxious and most desperate of the ringleaders, whom they removed for security to the neighbouring town of Rentworth.

It chanced that one of these ringleaders was wholly unconnected with the railway, although, as an amateur, he had warmly co-operated In the lawless proceedings of the mob. He belonged to the adjacent coal-mines; and news of his capture having reached the ears of the miners, who, as we have already stated, were at that time unfortunately out on strike, the more turbulent amongst them joined the crowd of navigators who were gathering together to effect a rescue. The whole dis-turbance might have been put down by the exercise of timely vigour and timely justice. A handful of infantry from the nearest depot, and an immediate payment of all debts due from the company, would have at once restored tranquillity in the district. But the reports sent to the Home Secretary and the Lord-Lieutenant, did not explain the real cause of the disturbance. It was simply stated that the coal-miners were in open riot, in a locality where there were no regular police to oppose a steady, cool front to the rioters. Orders came down by telegraph to call out three troops of yeomanry, and summon two companies of infantry to the scene of the disturbance.

It was on Friday afternoon that the riot began; and, though partially quelled by the special constables, it was rumoured that the miners were in commotion, and that a renewal of disturbances might be anticipated All night the town of Rentworth was in a state of much anxiety, and justly so; for before the military were well on the move, the mob, composed of navvies, Irish labourers, and miners, were pouring through the High Street of Rentworth, and in complete possession of the place.

Nugent, immediately he reached home, despatched messengers in all directions to hasten the muster of his troop, and busied himself in preparing his arms and ac-coutrements for the march. By dint of energy and activity, aided by the influence he possessed over that portion of the yeomanry under his command, these endeavours proved so far successful, that Nugent and about three-parts of his troop, tolerably well appointed and with horses still fresh, might be seen winding down the hill, at the foot of which lies the straggling town of Rentworth, just as the sun began to descend, broad and red, behind the dusky volumes of smoke overshadowing the tall chimneys and dimly-defined houses of the manufacturers and miners, to the west-ward of the town. As they approached the suburbs, a yeomanry officer, who acted as adjutant, rode up, and was immediately surrounded by the whole of Nugent's troop, clamouring for intelligence, and slightly oblivious of military discipline.

" Keep your ranks, pray, gentlemen !" shouted Nugent. " Keep your ranks I Fall into your places, gen-tlemen. Halt! Halt!",

Having restored order to his troop, Nugent once more gave the order to advance, and listened to the ad-jutant's recital of the events of the past night and day.

" Tis the old story of looking the stable door after the horse is stolen!" exclaimed the latter " Our two troops muster pretty strong; though the fellows grum-bled prodigiously at leaving their corn-fields. The Colonel had just got a touch of the gout again, and had to join us in his family coach. A pretty jolting it got over the hills! But he would push on, sitting in-. side in full regimentals, pitched from one seat to an-other, but looking as fierce as a lion. When we got in, our horses were quite spent, and the men ready to drop< The thing was all over, however; the prisoners rescued ; the constables hid in coal-cellars or under beds; and every window in the ' Swampshire Arms' smashed to' atoms !"

" And what has become of the mob ?"

" Oh! started somewhere else, or scattered about in the neighbourhood. We shall be off again, I expect, in a couple of hours.

"Are the soldiers arrived T"

"The infantry? yes, they axe in the market-place. Two companies, mustering about a hundred men, but a good many ale straggling. The rearguard is bringing them up."

"Well," said Nugent, "as we are to be off again, I shall keep my horses as fresh as I can."

"To be sure," said the other, "that's just what I was to advise you. Will'you take a cigar?"

The offer was declined, and once more halting his men, Nugent led them into

the town in good order, but - without that clang and animating clatter of horses*
hoofs and steel scabbards, which a brisk trot would have elicited. Little boys who
came out to cheer, seeing the stolid and demure procession, only stared with disappointed faces; and the men themselves seemed rather crestfallen at " sneaking," as
they observed, "into the town as if they were ashamed of themselves." Passing the
market-place, Nugent found the infantry had piled arms, and were dispersed in all
directions, , some seated on the ground, some on benches and stools brought them
from the market, regaling themselves on the rations they had carried with them.
A few were bathing their feces at the pump in the market-place, and drinking water with the eagerness of pilgrims in the desert. The men were covered with dust,
and had evidently executed a rapid and fatiguing march. A volley of questions and
answers was nevertheless vivaciously exchanged with the yeomanry as they passed
by, coupled with observations of rather a jocose description, which were tolerably
well received. On arriving at the " Swampshire arms," they found not only every
window smashed, but every thing which was fragile or easily destructible flung into
the street, or shivered to atoms. Much of the furniture had been wantonly broken,
and the banisters on the staircase hacked and split with knives and hatchets; but,
beyond this, there had been no further damage of consequence, for the operations
of the mob were interrupted by the approach of the troops. The officers of both
yeomanry and infantry were assembled in the principal room; seniors holding a sort
of council of war in the corner of the apartment; juniors eating bread and cheese
without plates, off a broken table, and drinking wine and water from a tin saucepan
without a handle. It appeared, according to the best information collected, that the
mob had fled in various directions with the intention of re-assembling at the mines
at nightfall, either for the purpose of further mischief or of indulging in triumphant
festivities. The colonel of the yeomanry was therefore eager to start for the mines
at once, in his family coach (which had not broken more than one spring In its
journey across the hills), and thus followed by his faithful troopers, to —" beard
the lion in his den, and nip the mischief in the bud." So said Colonel Plover of the
yeomanry. But the major commanding the regulars demurred to this proposal, and
recommended that scouts should be sent out first to gather information, and mean
time that men and horses should rest and refresh themselves.

Nugent had just begun to second the major's proposition when a great hubbub was heard below; shouting, trampling of feet, jingling of spurs, clattering of steel scabbards. Colonel Plover started to his feet, but a twinge of the gout sent him back again into his chair. The officers abandoned their bread and cheese, and seized their swords. But Johnson of the regulars, an old campaigner, who always had his wits about him, took this opportunity of quietly tossing off the remainder of the wine and water in the tin pot. The adjutant rushed out of the room to inquire what was the matter, and young Lord Swampshire, who commanded one of the troops of yeomanry, examined the caps of a small Colt's revolver he carried in his pocket.

Presently word was sent up that one of the rioters had been discovered hid in the back-kitchen of the inn, and was in custody below. An attempt was immediately made to give an air of judicial dignity to the apartment where the officers were congregated. Colonel Plover's chair was wheeled with its back to the fireplace, two or three of the largest chairs were placed on either side, and occupied by the senior officers. The table was pushed to one side of the room. Barclay Fitzomelette, a young yeomanry, officer of a romantic turn, suggested that the, effect would be enhanced by partially closing the shutters and darkening the room. But this was over-ruled. The ad-jutant produced several quires of foolscap and quill pens, with blotting-paper to match. Search was made for a Bible, in case it should be necessary to take any evidence on oath.

Mr. Rubbley, as a local magistrate, was summoned from his neighbouring mansion, the windows of which the mob had smashed early in the day. And the worthy magistrate, being discovered concealed in an empty wine-pipe in his cellar, was gently extracted therefrom and hurried to the " Swampshire Arms," smelling of port-wine in the most convivial manner possible, but with a face pale as ashes, and lugubriously sober.

Before his arrival, however, the door of the officers' apartment was flung open with some emphasis, and two dismounted yeomanry, huge men—six feet high or so-armed to the teeth, stalked solemnly into the room, dragging between them a small boy covered with soot, with his hair hanging over his eyes, and his clothes all torn and disordered. In the rear followed two infantry soldiers, with fixed bayonets, and muskets at half cock. The procession drew up at one end of the room and faced the colonel, whilst the yeomanry adjutant bustled about endeavouring to dress the troopers, the small prisoner, and the two regulars, in a correct line.

At this imposing spectacle the younger officers showed a rather indecorous inclination to laugh. Indeed, John-son dipped his head once more into the tin pot, for the purpose, as he afterwards declared, of hiding his merriment. The striking diminution in the sherry induced, however, the other officers to suspect that this was only a partial explanation of the manoeuvre.

"Where did you discover the prisoner? " inquired Colonel Plover, rising with some difficulty, and supporting himself with one hand on his sword, and the other on a gold-headed cane, an heirloom of the Plover family. " Where did you discover the prisoner ? "

"We found him, please your honour—beg your honours pardon, colonel I should have said—in the kitchen copper."

"Copper, copper? " And the colonel shook his head as if he thought the matter was really becoming serious. "Found him in the copper? What the deuce was fie doing there? Eh?"

" Seemed to be a-hiding of his self, please your honour, —colonel I should have said. You see it happened as thus :—Tom Harness, he was agoing"

"Who's Tom Harness, sir?" inquired the colonel with a stern voice, anxious to impress the regulars with a profound idea of the discipline maintained in his corps— "Who's Tom Harness ? Eh, sir ? "

"Why, bless your honour—colonel I should say-he's your honour's pig-butche down at Saltmaxah! Thought your honour know'd he as well ye know'd me, saving your honour's presence!"

The officers tittered convulsively. The colonel reddened, and shouted, " Go on, sir! You're a long time getting to the point. Go on, sir!"

" Well, you see's we was going to light a bit of fire, having a mind for a sup of hot tea. So we got some sticks together and had just struck a light, when who should pop up out of the copper, sending the cover spinning into the midst of us, but this here young scamp!"

And the trooper gave the boy a roughish shake, just to explain who he was referring to.

At this point of the narrative there was another titter amongst the officers, and Johnson was so much overcome as to be forced to bury his face in the tin pot for at least a minute.

" That gave thee a start, Simpson, I'll be bound!" remarked a yeomanry officer of elderly appearance, a very red face, and rather round shoulders.

"Why, squire—captain I should say—I'll not deny we were taken aback for a bit. 'I was for all the world like Jack in the box, or Guy Faux, or some such a thing!"

"You need not pull the boy about in that way," remonstrated Nugent, perceiving that he was oscillating to and fro under the grasp of the two troopers, who laboured under the impression that each movement they alternately imparted to the little figure between them, was some refractory effort on his part to escape.

" Let the prisoner stand by himself," said the colonel with an air of gracious condescension. " We will give him a trial. If he attempts to escape, seize him again and hold him fast!"

" Ah, colonel, he's a downright bad 'un, you may be sure!" replied Simpson, reluctantly leaving go of the boy's collar.

Colonel Plover having retreated, with the help of his sword and stick, to the further corner of the room, con-ferred a few minutes with the infantry major, and then turning round, exclaimed—

" Guard!"

"Yes, please your honour!" exclaimed the two troopers clutching tightly hold again of the boy's jacket with simultaneous energy. " Yes, colonel!"

" Leave the prisoner with us, and retire."

" You may withdraw!" added the adjutant.

" But keep within hail!" put in the red-faced yeomanry officer,

" Keep within hail, Simpson!" echoed Barclay Fitz-omelette, in a melo-dramat-ic whisper.

" You may go, Simpson!" exclaimed all the officers in chorus, dutifully backing up their colonel.

The two infantry, rank and file, had shouldered arms and faced to the right, and were half-way down-stairs before Simpson and his comrade had shut their mouths expanded to the widest extent by the unlooked-for command of their colonel.

" Hadn't we better search him colonel ?" exclaimed at length Simpson. " He might have something dangerous about him."

"Well, well, search him then," rather pettishly replied the chief.

" Sharp fellow, that Simpson!" whispered the red-faced officer to the adjutant.

The ceremony was duly performed, and the contents of the boy's pockets placed upon the table, namely—an old clasp-knife, three marbles, and a decayed apple.

" That will do. Now you may go, sir."

The troopers trudged off, casting mistrustful glances at the boy, who stood perfectly motionless in the middle of the room.

" Well, my little man, what's your name, and where do you come from ? "

There was a long pause, and at length the boy answered—

" I come from the copper in the back kitchen."

The colonel, in a fine purple glow of official wrath, looked round to his brother officers, and asked—

" Does the little scamp mean to be impertinent, or is he a fool"

"More knave than fool," observed the red-faced officer, with the round shoulders.

"May be he's frightened," suggested the infantry major.

" Colonel," [interrupted Captain Pinkie, a bustling yeomanry officer, who endeavoured to hold his head in military fashion, but only looked as if some one had just given him a little jerk under the nose from which it had not yet recovered. "Colonel," said Captain Pinkie, pushing forwards, "this is a 'sort' I think I know how to manage, and by your leave I'll tackle him,'

So saying he strode up to the boy, and in a loud sharp voice exclaimed—

" Young rogue, I say! What's thy name ? Eh, young rogue ? "

" I'm no more a rogue than thou art," answered the boy sullenly.

"I think," interrupted the colonel, who had been whispering with the infantry major—" I think there are too many of us here. Pinkie, you had better let the' boy alone. The adjutant will talk to him, or perhaps Captain Nugent," he added, as Nugent, who had left the' room to speak to one of his troop, at that moment re-entered it. " Why, the boy starts as if he knew you name, Captain Nugent!"

Nugent immediately led the lad outside the door, and was about to put some questions to him, when, to his surprise, the boy began the conversation himself

"Squire Nugent, please, don't let them shoot me! I have done nobody any hurt. I haven't indeed, Squire Nugent."

" Why, my boy, who are you ? What's your name ?"

" I'm Edward—Edward Harrill. Don't you remember me and Margaret?"

The boy vainly tried to wipe the soot and tears from his face in order that Nugent might recognize him. But Nugent now knew him by his voice and manner, and, taking his hand, told him he need not be afraid, only he must tell the truth. The boy then began to take courage, and told Nugent all he knew.

It appeared that Harrill for some weeks past had kept the boy at his lodging at Rentworth, to cook for him and wait upon him, threatening him with awful punishment if he attempted to abscond. As soon as the miners were in commotion, and the riots began in the streets of Rentworth, Harrill speedily took the lead in all the mischief going forwards, and joined the mob, taking Edward with him to prevent his escaping. Whilst the rioters were smashing the windows and the furniture of the " Swampshire Arms," a cry arose that " The soldiers were coming!" There was a general panic, and in the confusion Edward slipped out of Harrill's sight, and hid himself in the empty copper of. the back kitchen, where he lay crouched in great approtension, both on account of Harrill and on account of the soldiers.'

After a long interval of silence, and when he was getting almost exhausted, he heard afresh tumult overhead, and presently the trampling of feet in all directions, and some men came into the kitchen, and began to kindle a fire directly beneath the copper. Then, not liking the idea of being fried alive, he jumped up, and frightened the yeomanry out of their wits. They took him for some fiendish sprite, and made for the door, tumbling over the chairs and tables in their way. Here they met one of the infantry, and, roused to a feeling of profes-sional emulation, they returned to the charge, and seeing the boy had emerged from the copper, and was sitting quietly in the ashes, the whole party chivalrously rushed upon him and called upon him to " surrender," which he instantaneously did. This was the substance of the boy's statement, and Nugent felt satisfied that he told the simple truth.

"But, my boy, do you know where the mob are bound to now? Do you know if they are dispersed,.or gone elsewhere ? "

" Oh yes I They are off over the moor! They are going to burn all the houses of the folk that have got' the railway money."

" Whom do you mean, boy ?" asked Nugent anxiously.

" I don't know what folk they meant. The directors, they called 'em. But I know where they are gone. They are oyer the moor to Beaumont-house, and Harrill's with them."

The next moment Nugent rushed into the room where the officers were assem-bled, and exclaimed with more agitation than he was wont to evince—" Gentlemen, I know this boy, and can trust him. He states that the mob have re-assembled in the outskirts of the town, and have started across the marshes to Beaumont-house, the seat, as you are aware, of Mr. Usherwood, one of the directors of the railway. No doubt they are up to some mischief. We must follow on their track, or we do not know what may happen."

There was much excitement Young Lord Swamp-shire brandished his revolv-er, to the serious discomfort of the red-feced officer, who said he didn't want to be made cold meat of before his time. Pinkie pranced about the room, trying to buckle his sword-belt. The adjutant rushed up to Colonel Plover, and as the colonel at the same instant rose to meet him, they fell into each other's arms, as if in a paroxysm of confiding affection. Johnson, the old campaigner, vanished out of the room to join his men. The infantry major leaned out of the broken window, and, calling the bugler, told him to sound the " assembly."

Nugent, as soon as the bustle permitted, again spoke. " Colonel Plover and Ma-jor West, my troop is pretty fresh, both men and horses, and I know the country well. Shall I start at once, in pursuit of the rioters across the moor? Pinkie and Lord Swampshire can bring their men on afterwards."

The infantry major approved, and said he would, if the colonel approved, pick out a score of his best men, and send them in the same direction in any light carts or vehicles they might be able to procure.

" And let me advise you, Captain Nugent, to clap that young gentleman, your prisoner, in front of a trooper, and take him along with you."

In a few minutes the town was once more in commotion. Bugles and trumpets blowing, horsemen clattering over the stones, soldiers running to and fro, officers shouting, two carbines of the yeomanry going off by accident but fortunately not doing any injury, the colonel calling for his coach at the pitch of his voice with as much vehemence as King Richard called for a horse. Then the measured tramp of infantry was heard along the street, and presently afterwards Nugent and his troop emerged from the inn-yard, and clattered down the street at a full trot, eliciting screams of applause from the boys of the town, especially when they detected Ed-ward Harrill's small form perched in front of one of the leading troopers.

It is not easy to bring fifty or sixty horsemen, with heavy accoutrements and ammunition, at a quick pace for several miles together along an indifferent road. The yeomanry horses were unaccustomed to work of this description. Many were much distressed before half the journey was accomplished, and the best-mounted troopers had to hold back, in order to favour their less fortunate companions. The mob had obtained a good start, and improved it by taking a short cut across the fields soon after leaving the mines, which had the further advantage of rendering the point of their destination uncertain. The yeomanry had to march ten miles by the road. Those they pursued reduced their journey to only eight miles, by the angle they thus cut off. Nugent urged on his men, and tried to keep up their spirits. The men in his troop had confidence in him, and followed his directions with alacrity. It was not long before they came upon traces of the mob; stragglers were occasionally seen escaping over the fields; here and there a pick-axe or bludgeon had been dropped in the road; the fields on either side had been in places trampled down, and fences torn and broken.

Then they came upon country folks who gave a vivid picture of the insolent fury of the rioters; then they passed a beer-shop which had been pillaged, and all the liquor on the premises drunk or poured into the ditch. Here they captured half a score of the rioters lying dead drunk about the premises. These they left in charge of three or four yeomanry, selecting those whose horses were most knocked up. At length the foremost troopers reached a sharp turn in the road, from whence an extensive view of the open country, as well as the long range of hilly ground beyond, could be obtained. At this point a lane turned off, leading to the Manor-house Farm by a more direct route than the road passing Beaumont-house.

"Master," exclaimed Madocks, who was a private in Nugent's troop; " Master, d'ye see that terrible smoke yonder?"

It was in the direction of Okenham valley, and arose in huge volumes, sometimes dark, sometimes lurid red.

D'ye see, master—d'ye see ? " urged the man, who was on a sudden pale with anxiety.

There was a burst of exclamations from the troopers, as one after another they caught sight of the conflagration.

Nugent said composedly—

"Madocks, it is our stack-yard. It is just in the bend of the hill; there's no doubt about it But it can't be helped.

" We had best turn off at the cross roads, and make straight for the farm' suggested Madocks,

"No, Madocks, our duty is straightforwards towards the point agreed upon. It is plain the bulk of the mob is still before us. Forwards! if you please, gentlemen," cried Nugent more loudly, as several of the yeomanry began to pull up at the cross roads, manifestly expecting Nugent's orders to turn towards the farm. " Forwards! forwards to Beaumont-house!" He galloped to the front, and his troop followed.

"Can that young urchin have *done* us, sir?" asked Madocks, again overtaking him. " Was he left to put us on a wrong scent ?"

Nugent felt for a moment a painful suspicion cross his mind. " Bring him to the front !" he said.

The trooper who carried the boy rode to the front. Nugent sternly questioned him; but the boy remained firm and unflinching. Opinions were divided as to his guilt or innocence. Still they pushed on, and now, as they neared the park of Beaumont-house, could just discern upon the rising ground groups of men, clustering and thronging together, as if watching their approach.

"Keep together, gentlemen—draw swords!" and, as the steel flashed in the air, the horses seemed to share their masters' excitement, and pressed forwards with a less stiff and mechanical motion. Nugent still headed them.

In the distance he saw his ricks and premises— perhaps his house—enveloped in flames and smoke. But he had no thought of swerving from his purpose. Two motives governed him. First, a sense of duty; next, a tender anxiety on Gertrude's account. Nevertheless there was no undue precipitation, or impetuous hurry in his movements. He held his men well together, and advanced with sufficient rapidity, but without confusion or disorder.

CHAPTER IX.

PASSAGE IN THE LIFE OF A RAILWAY DIRECTOR.

THE morning of the day on which the yeomanry were summoned to Rentworth, Lady Maud sat in the break-fast-room with a countenance unusually serene. Gertrude was late that day, and her ladyship and Mr. Usher-wood were téte-à-téte.

" My love," said Lady Maud, holding up two letters she had in her hand, " I have some satisfactory intelligence for you to-day."

" Glad to hear it," rejoined her husband. " It is high time something pleasant turned up. Just by way of variety. I'm fond of variety." He uttered these words in a tone of despondency unusual with him. For since his first introduction to the reader a good deal of alteration might have been noticed in Mr. Usherwood's general aspect and demeanour. He was not only thinner and his brow more wrinkled, but he looked restless, feverish, and excited. At the moment his wife spoke to him, he crammed two or three unopened letters into his pocket. He had lately fallen into the inconvenient habit of postponing to read his letters for days, and sometimes for weeks.

" Ah, my dear!" exclaimed Lady Maud, " you are still brooding over those horrid railways ! That I see clearly. Now, pray don't think of the share-market just now. Put it away in some little snug corner of your mind. After all, we know how much we have invested. We cannot lose more, and that will not ruin us. Banish the whole subject, love. This morning I have heard from my dear friend, Miss Hawkshaw. She informs me of the death of poor young Clinton. I am sorry for him." And Lady Maud's beautiful eyes seemed for a moment almost moistened. " Cut off in his prime!" Then added more cheerfully—" and there is a note from Sir Eliot Prichard. Satisfactory, but a little perplexing. Bead it, dear!"

Mr. Usherwood, having fortified his nerves by two or three cups of strong coffee, took the letter which Lady Maud held out to him, but with a trembling hand. It was the way with him now, he said, whenever he received a fresh letter, whatever its contents were. The letter was long, but might have been compressed into a very few lines; the purport being that Sir Eliot was profoundly affected by Miss Usherwood's rare intellectual qualities and amiable disposition. As for her personal charms, though of the most dazzling order, these were of secondary importance in his eyes. He begged, therefore, through the medium of her natural guardians and protectors, to throw himself at her feet as the humblest but sincerest of her admirers, and propose himself as a candidate for her hand.

" Well," said Mr. Usherwood,- putting his hand to his brow, " so far, so good. But my little girl may not fancy him. And, besides, I thought you had fixed upon Mr. Nugent. Is he to be turned adrift again, after all the trouble you have taken ? "

"My dear," replied Lady Maud, in a tone of gentle reproof, "you mistake. My trouble has been very insignificant. We have only shown civility to Mr. Nugent, as the probable representative of a powerful and wealthy family. I restricted myself to the most cautious ad-vances. I did not wish any thing decisive to take place. It might have been premature and embarrassing. *Now* the case is different; but I could wish poor Clinton had postponed his decease a few weeks longer."

" And what are we to do with Sir Eliot ? " asked her husband.

"Why, we must consider about it, and feel our way a little. He is a suitable match. Clever, rich, not ill-looking, if he would plaster down that woolly black hair of his, and roll his eyes rather less. But, then, you see his fortune is nothing to the Clinton property, and Nugent is twice as presentable a man, agriculturist though he be."

" Which of the two does our little girl like best ?" asked Mr. Usherwood.

" Why, I have my private impression upon that point. But we must not be in a hurry."

"Let me see Miss Hawkshaw's letter,'

"Wait an instant, I have not finished reading it myself yet."

And Lady Maud, opening the letter, recommended reading it with an air of tranquil interest. Suddenly, the languid expression of her countenance changed to a look of impatience, almost of anger. She threw down the letter and exclaimed, " What a tiresome, provoking woman! I give her up entirely."

" What's the matter? " asked her husband.

"Why, only think. She adds in a postscript at the end, that 'tis *old* Clinton—old Sir Lawrence—who is dead, and not his son. And what. is more, she says, the common opinion is, Sir Regmald is much better, and will recover!"

" Is it possible ?" rejoined Mr. Usherwood. " Well, poor fellow, we ought to be glad of it, and I really am glad. But I wish he would not keep us in such villainous uncertainty, but would do one thing or the other."

" The old gentleman could not stand the climate of Nice. In fact he was told as much, so Miss Hawk-shaw says; but he ***would*** accompany his son, and now he is gone, and the son is doing well. How strange is human life!"

Lady Maud drank her tea very slowly, as if philosophically meditating on the occurrence, and desirous of regaining her composure.

" One thing is clear "—she added at last—" Nugent sinks into an ineligible farmer."

" He's a good fellow, too," observed Mr. Usherwood. " So clever at all sorts of things. We never got any ice better than dirty snow until he had our ice-house reconstructed. And then the hot-houses, what a glorious improvement he made there ! Only think of the pines we had, Maud—only think of the pines!" And the old gentleman smacked his lips at the recollection. of them.

" Yes, my dear, that's all very true—perfectly true; in fact, almost affecting. But it is nothing to the point. When business is on the tapis, we must postpone sentiment."

Mr. Usherwood yielded with humility, and dived into the recesses of an egg.

"My dear," proceeded Lady Maud, " I fear we must fall back upon Sir Eliot Prichard."

"Well, he's clever—decidedly clever, I must say, though he does advocate the abolition of capital punishment. My throat would not be safe an hour!" added the old gentleman, swallowing half an egg at once, as if to assure himself that as yet all was right in that direction. " Murders would be as plentiful as common assaults. We should have shops, with ' murders neatly executed' placarded in the windows, and advertisements hawked about, headed ' Important to the public ! Male and female slaughterhouse opened at the back of Smithfield. No questions asked. Children half price!'"

"Well, my dear, I am glad to see you in such spirits."

Mr. Usherwood laughed, but in a guttural, excited way, as if he did not enjoy it.

" Well, I am really rejoiced you are so particularly merry, my dear. But, to re-turn to Sir Eliot——"

" Clever man, but of dangerous views," interrupted her husband.

"My own love," said Lady Maud, with the smallest approach of fretfulnese in her accents—" my own darling, never mind his views. What do you think of hint as a husband?—as a husband for our dear child?"

" Hum—Lady Prichard ? I mean—beg your pardon, Sir Eliot, beg your pardon humbly," said Mr. Usher-wood, bowing his head towards the fireplace with gro-tesque reverence—" I mean Lady Eliot Prichard. Sir Eliot and Lady Eliot Prichard! It's not what you call a pretty name—is it, my love ? "

" There is nothing," continued his lady abstractedly— " nothing to be objected to on the score of fortune, family (there's a hitch about Sir Eliot's grandmother but that's ages ago, and there was a market gardener on the maternal grandfather's side but that's not gene-rally known)—family, personal appearance, or mind. He was wild, but young men will be wild, and that is all past."

" But," exclaimed Mr. Usherwood, throwing himself suddenly back in his chair, and again putting his hand to his head, " the grand point is this. Does my little girl care for him ? I don't say, does she love him, my dear, but does she not dislike him ? "

" For that," resumed Lady Maud, " we must give her time. There must be no unnecessary fuss or hurry. There is no cause for it"

Rising from the breakfast table, they left the room.

"My dear," said Lady Maud, shutting the door behind them, and putting her arm gently in his, "You seem to me a little out of sorts. I don't think you are quite well. I wish you would have a few minutes' chat with Grierson."

"No, I thank ye, Maud—no, I thank ye. Lady Eliot Prichard. Prichard ? What an odd name! Sir Eliot Prichard ! Lady Eliot Prichard !"

And, laughing to himself, Mr. Usherwood walked heavily towards the library, muttering the word " Prichard " between his teeth in every variety of intonation, as if each time it presented quite a new aspect to his mind.

Lady Maud looked after him with an expression of perplexity in her countenance.

" He certainly has altered. Grierson must see him. Grierson must positively see him, this very day!"

She then betook herself to her usual matutinal rendezvous with Mrs. Millet the housekeeper; but somehow or other evinced less composure and self-possession than was her wont. In fact, Lucy Weston, who had recently returned to service at Beaumont-house, intimated respectfully to Gertrude, whilst she was assisting at her toilette, that she was sure something had gone wrong, for "My lady is in such a way! Not but what," she added, " Paine and Mrs. Millet are as much as flesh and blood can bear—but I' never saw my lady so sharp upon them. Something's gone wrong, for a certainty."

Gertrude blushed, as if she felt a misgiving she had something to do with the unwonted acerbity of her mother's manner.

At that precise moment a loud sob was heard at the door, and then an agitated knock.

" Lucy—see who's there," said Gertrude.

"'Tis Miss Beverley, ma'am," was the maid's reply as she opened the door, and the governess entered the room in rather a hurried way, and with very red eyes.

"What *is* the matter?" cried Gertrude.

"Nothing," said Miss Beverley, glancing at the maid as if she considered her at that moment decidedly *de trap*. As, however, Lucy did not accept the hint, but only responded by a gentle toss of the head, Gertrude, being now ready to descend, took Miss Beverley's arm, and, leaving the room together, they withdrew to Miss Beverley's apartment.

" What is the matter, dear ?" again inquired Gertrude.

"It is of no consequence," answered the other. "I am used to the finger of scorn, and the hissing accents of contempt. I take these things—quietly—now; very —quietly," and, giving utterance to these sentiments in disjointed words, Miss Beverley began to sob,

"Pray, explain yourself," urged Gertrude. "Who has ever treated you with scorn in this house ? Have I? Has any body?"

" Scorn is the portion of the governess! Petty insult, her daily bread ! I ought not to complain."

And Miss Beverley, with a show of fortitude, pushed a table covered with the remains of an excellent break-fast out of the way, and sat down in a luxurious arm-chair, holding herself resolutely upright, as if she was sitting upon some cushion-less, three-legged stool.

" Hardships are my lot!" she added, enunciating the syllables with an emphasis which imparted an oscillating movement to the patent spring-cushion upon which she sat, and a corresponding vibration to her whole person —" Hardships are my lot!"

"I must really run and get some breakfast," said Gertrude, who was growing impatient as well as hungry. Miss Beverley's manner underwent a total metamorphosis.

"Oh, my dear, darling, good Gertrude ! I thought you had had your breakfast—I did, really! How selfish I was! Forgive me—pray, forgive me!"

And, so saying, she sprang up from the spring cushion, and would have hurried Gertrude out of the room; but the latter declared she would breakfast off the remains of Miss Beverley's repast, and listen to the recital of her woes meantime.

It was with rather diminished excitement that Miss Beverley, whilst Gertrude sipped her lukewarm tea, proceeded to narrate that Lady Maud came into the schoolroom that morning, and, after finding fault with the French themes and every thing on the table, went to the window and stood looking out at the distant hills. Whereupon Miss Beverley, who thought the silence awkward, merely observed that 'twas a pity Gertrude did not ride so much now, and intimated that Mr. Nugent was very remiss not to have ridden with her lately.

"On this Lady Maud looked round at me," said Miss Beverley—growing rather warm at the recollection —" looked round at me, as if I had been a mere worm, or earwig, or something equally unpleasant and contemptible, and, making a very long neck, said, ' I do not wish, Miss Beverley, that you should couple Miss Usherwood's name with the name of any gentleman who may chance to obtain the honour of her acquaintance. I don't blame you. You mean it kindly. But let me beg you will be more circumspect.' And BO saying, your mamma bowed to me, and sailed out of the room as if I was a street-sweeper to whom she had refused an alms. It is hard after all my troubles and my exertions !"

What further would have been said, and how Gertrude—whom this recital had a little discomposed— would have consoled her companion, we cannot say; for at that moment a solemn tap at the door was heard, and Paine proclaimed, in an impressive whisper through the keyhole, that her ladyship desired to speak with Miss Usherwood "directly," and the conference terminated.

Lady Maud, when Gertrude entered her boudoir, was seated near the window, with some open letters, an account-book, and a file or two of bills on a table near her. She looked more serious than usual, and there was a restlessness about her eye which denoted she was not quite at ease.

" Gertrude, my sweet child," she began, " I have a few words to say to you, if you are quite disengaged."

Gertrude sat down on a low stool by her mother's side, without any reply, but with a beating heart.

"Time flies fast, dearest," proceeded her mother, " Let me see, you were eighteen last spring."

" Yes, mamma, in May "

"I was seventeen when I married your father," continued Lady Maud in a meditative mood. " Our family were famous for early marriages. The Countess of Delafield (my lamented grandmother) was still at school when the Earl proposed; and as for my dear mother, it was generally believed she concealed a doll in her trunk when she started for her wedding tour on the continent."

Lady Maud paused, and Gertrude wondered whither these remarks were tending. Lady Maud resumed rather abruptly, "Have you ridden lately with Sir Eliot, my dear?"

"Not very lately—I am not so fond of riding as I was."

" It is dull riding without a companion," rejoined her mother. " I am vexed there is so little society in this neighbourhood. We must make the most of what we have, however; for in the reduced state of your father's finances, a season in town is this year out of the question."

Gertrude had heard some dark hints on the subject of embarrassed income and pecuniary difficulties. Of Course she understood very little, and thought less about the matter; but her mother's countenance and manner were to-day so unusually grave in alluding to the subject, that Gertrude felt a vague anxiety steal over her mind.

" Economy has become a duty, and yet how dangerous an one! It excites disagreeable suspicions, and often precipitates a crisis that might have been averted, or at least postponed. I should be happy, come what may proceeded Lady Maud, her eyes becoming tearful— " I should be at peace if I could see my daughters advantageously and suitably settled before undeserved distress embittered their young hearts!"

Gertrude knelt by her mother's side, and, fondly caressing her, declared that she ought not to think about them; that if they were all of them together in however humble a home, they would be happy. " And you especially, my dearest," continued her mother, gently settling her bracelet and rings, which had been disarranged by her daughter's caresses, and putting Gertrude's collar strait, but all the while in tears— " You, my dearest, I do wish to see united to a man I can trust and esteem; to one possessed of competent fortune and unblemished name I"

Gertrude tried to laugh it off as a joke, but succeeded very badly.

" My sweet, how you tremble! Kiss me, child, and do not agitate yourself needlessly. One would suppose you expected to be married tomorrow I"

" Dearest mother, I am in no impatience for such an event, believe me. I am very happy as I am."

Lady Maud sighed, and taking up a letter appeared to cast her eye over the contents, then, bending down over her daughter, said, "Don't flurry yourself, my child. Let us turn to another subject. Will you drive with us to-day to call on the Clairs?"

" Mamma," said Gertrude, rather agitated, " I know you have something more to say to me. I had rather hear it all, and have it over.*

" No, darling, no! There is no need to say more at present. If I had thought you would have been so excited, I should not have broached the subject."

" Pray, tell me all, mamma. Do not leave me in suspense."

" Poor child," replied her mother, stroking Gertrude's flushed cheek, " you are quite in a fever! You must learn to take these things quietly. I had had three proposals at your age, and you have had none yet. At least," she added, glancing at her daughter with a look of gradually dawning suspicion—" At least as far as I am aware; as far as the amount of confidence you have placed in me enables me to judge."

" Dearest mother I" interrupted Gertrude in a deprecating tone of voice.

"My love, it may be best to let you know at once, that there is one not far from this neighbourhood to whom you are not indifferent."

Gertrude hid her face in her mother's lap, not knowing what was coming next, but hoping for the best,

Lady Maud, with a slight degree of anxiety in her voice and looks, proceeded:—

" In fact, your father and I have this very day received a letter from the person I allude to, begging our sanction for making a formal offer."

Gertrude did not move her head, but her heart beat more rapidly.

" There is no occasion, of course, for an immediate decision. Very possibly it will take you by surprise. It will be the wisest course to act towards him as if he had made no confession of his feelings, and you were simply on those friendly terms which near neighbours in a rather out-of-the-way part of the country ought to be."

There was a pause, but presently Lady Maud began again—

" Of course, darling, if you *should* contract an union which, I may as well admit, both your father and myself sincerely desire—if ever this should take place, your lot would be cast in quite a different sphere. A brilliant position in the first circles of London society, diversified by visits to the most interesting countries on the Continent, and an occasional sojourn at a luxurious country seat. Such a routine of existence would undoubtedly present an agreeable contrast to your way of life at Beaumont-house—which, I am free to confess, is not far removed from that of a vegetable. Associated with a husband, possessed of mind as well as heart—and let me incidentally observe, my dear Gertrude, that the man of mind commonly improves upon acquaintance, whereas the mere man of feeling sooner or later palls like an insipid sweetmeat—associated, I say, with such a husband as Sir Eliot Prichard"

Gertrude had hitherto listened, her head reclining on her mother's lap, with tolerable composure to this long address delivered by Lady Maud rapidly, but with distinct emphasis. When, however, she heard the name Sir Eliot, she could no longer contain herself, but, springing to her feet, exclaimed—

" Mother, I cannot bear him! I detest him! I wish he had never been born !"

Lady Maud gazed upon her with unaffected amazement. Accustomed to govern, either by the exercise of authority or by judicious management, those who were connected with her, she was unprepared for such a display of self-will and impetuosity in any of her own children, who, she had supposed, needed no more stringent influence than that imparted through the medium of Miss Beverley. But the very consciousness of Lady Maud's long-established authority added intensity to Gertrude's dismay and trouble of mind. Knowing well her mother's power, as well as her own weakness, she rose against it with a kind of desperate audacity. The next moment she sank into a chair, half alarmed at her vehemence; and, yielding to a rush of bitter despondency, could with difficulty restrain her tears. For (one little moment Lady Maud's blue eyes quivered with displesure, but it passed like a flash of summer lightning. She rose, stopped for one moment to gaze upon her child's face which trembled with conflicting emotions, and then leaning over her, kissed her forehead, pressed her to her bosom, and soothingly said, " There, there, darling, I have been over hasty. You shall have your own way. Be sure that you shall not be forced to take a step you secretly abhor."

Gertrude's tears now found free egress.

" My child," added Lady Maud, regarding her closely for a moment, "your affections are elsewhere fixed.

You have given away your heart, or at least you believe so!"

Gertrude's lips murmured some inarticulate words.

"But consider," proceeded her mother—"Does not your heart revolt against succumbing to a passion for one far inferior to yourself in rank, in station, in refinement of mind ? You shake your head ! But forgive me, dearest, if I press you further. Does not your maidenly delicacy shrink with horror from nourishing a sentiment that is wholly unrequited ? "

" Mamma," exclaimed Gertrude, whose feelings were without difficulty probed and laid bare by one so experienced in such investigations as her mother— " Mamma, it is not true!"

"Not true!" replied her mother; "What do you mean ? What do you know of Mr. Nugent's feelings t"

" Mamma!" replied Gertrude, with sudden energy, " he loves me! Indeed he does! He told me so himself. He was to come here this morning to talk it all over with you. No doubt he will soon be here. I wished for him to tell you first, but no concealment was intended. He—is—very—much—attached—to me."

And poor Gertrude, to speak plain language, began to cry.

The summer lightning played fitfully for an instant in Lady Maud's blue eyes, She took a turn up and down the room, as if to command her feelings. Then stopped suddenly, and said in a low, almost quiet voice Poor child! And when, may I venture to ask, did you come to this understanding ?"

"Yesterday," sobbed Gertrude.

" Yesterday! Only yesterday! And that accounted for your being so late. You met him, I suppose ? Yes, yes, of course."

A few minutes of silence passed, and then Lady Maud embraced her daughter affectionately, but gravely.

"Do not leave the house, dearest," she said; " I may want you again. You will be glad to be alone. Go, and bathe those poor, swollen eyes; and remember, we must be patient—all of us. If bitter disappointment be in store for your poor father and myself, I fear, dearest, that you too will have your trial to bear. We must comfort and support one another."

And, embracing her daughter once more, she dismissed her, and, seating herself by the window, leant her head upon her hand in deep thought. Then rising, and murmuring to herself—" I can scarcely blame her, but it is much to be regretted," she hastily quitted the apartment, and made the best of her way to the library.

She paused with her hand on the door to recover breath, having run down-stairs more rapidly than usual, and heard the sound of some one breathing heavily, as if in a deep but oppressive slumber.— "Poor fellow!" said Lady Maud—"He is asleep, I must not wake him." And she opened the door very gently, in order not to rouse her husband.

The library was a well-lighted sunny room, having a large bow-window at one end. When Lady Maud entered however it was partially darkened, the large window curtain of red damask having been let down. Mr. Usherwood had lately found the light too much for his eyes. Before, however, Lady Maud could distinctly take in all the objects in the room, she felt a cold chill strike her, as if there was something, she knew not what, amiss. It crept through her instan-taneously, and independently of any intelligence through the ordinary senses. The next moment a sudden scream burst from her lips. Upon the rug, in front of an arm-chair from which he seemed to have slid down, lay her husband stretched at full length, apparently in a state of stupor. Lady Maud was not a woman merely to stand still and scream. She rushed to the bell, rang it with all her force, threw open the window, and, kneeling down by her husband, untied his cravat and collar, and allowed the air from outside to play upon his head and face. The thought rushed through her mind amidst all her terror and anguish, that there was One whom in her prosperity she had too little regarded; One to whom now in the bitterness of her soul she would fain cry, and cry with all her strength, but feared it would be in vain. For how could she, who had not sought Him whilst all was well with her, expect He would be with her in the day of her calamity ?

All this passed in far less time than it takes to describe. In a few seconds the room was full of servants, wild with alarm and perplexity. The slamming of doors, the ringing of bells, and by and bye the sobs of women and children, broke the still-ness of the house. Lady Maud, herself, was now calm. She directed that her husband should be carried to his bedroom, and de-spatched the servants for medical aid. As she went to and fro, she met Gertrude standing pale and trembling in the passage, and eager to be of some use. She kissed her, and said hastily—

" Go, dear—go and comfort your poor sisters; tell them I trust your father will soon be better. The doctor has been sent for." Gertrude returned to the. schoolroom, and endeavoured to console her sisters as well as she could. She thought she would read to them out of the Bible, Her mind instinctively turned to that source of peace and comfort, which as yet, it is to be feared, she had regarded too much in the light of a mere lesson-book.

Miss Beverley had gone to pay a visit to Mrs. Clair's governess, and had locked up all the school-room Bibles and prayer-books. So Gertrude ran to her room, and fetched the ornamented church service-book her mother had a few months ago presented to her. Sitting down, and drawing Agatha and Jessie to either side, she read one of the psalms with a faltering voice, whilst the gaudy decorations surrounding the page were wetted by her tears.

Meantime Lady Maud, having done what she could for her unconscious husband, returned to the library. Something seemed to have occurred to her mind. She drew up the crimson curtains, through which the sun now cast a sanguine glare, and making her way across the room amidst articles of furniture displaced in the recent confusion, snatched from the table, near the chair where her husband had been seated, several letters that looked as if they had been freshly torn open. One of them, dated a day or two back, was from a railway director, urging Mr. Usherwood's attendance at the meeting of the committee of inquiry into the affairs of the Rentworth line. He must have kept it in his pocket unopened through fear of the contents. Another contained a concise abstract of the labours of the committee, hastily drawn up, exposing the disastrous condition of the company, and stating the disappearance of the parties principally responsible for the liabilities incurred; whilst his attendance at the sitting of the committee was again urged upon him. Then there was a hastily scrawled note from the acting secretary, briefly describing the riots of the day before, and stating the necessity of funds being immediately raised for the discharge of all the more pressing and important claims upon the company. This correspondence was of a grave character; but it was followed by a letter which gave Lady Maud more uneasiness than all she had hitherto read It was from their solicitor, and in it there was distinct allusion to certain moneys invested in the Three per Cents., which it was intended to settle upon their children. From the tenor of the solicitor's letter, it appeared that the sum in question had been, unknown to Lady Maud, sold out of the funds, and employed to meet the calls made by the railway company upon the holders of their shares.

Severe as was this fresh blow, it was far less acutely felt by Lady Maud, at the present juncture, than would have been the case if all had been as usual in the house. Now, with her husband lying in dangerous illness, the loss of income sank into comparative insignificance. She turned almost with a sense of nausea from matters of business and of money. Nevertheless it seemed highly probable that the unfavourable intelligence contained in the letters she had just read, was in part the occasion of her husband's sudden and alarming attack. Locking up the letters she left the room, and once more ascended to the bedroom of the sick man.

In the mean time, the coachman had saddled a horse and started at a gallop for Mr. Grierson. Finding him from home he set off in pursuit, and, after tracing him from place to place, at length overtook him near the union workhouse at Flintwood. He was in his gig, and, in order to save time, John proposed his mounting the horse he was riding himself. To this Mr. Grierson acceded; and, leaving John to follow in his gig, sprang up on the horse and was soon out of sight. John followed at first at a sober pace, but presently, growing anxious to hear how his master was, gently urged Mr. Grierson's horse forward. On passing Mr. Lovell's parsonage, he observed the rector in close conversation with his old gardener, devising, as it would seem, some sort of horticultural employment for half a dozen stoat urchins from the national school, whom, as it was holiday week, Lovell wished to keep out of mischief.

The gardener eyed them with extreme suspicion, and as he occasionally turned up a good clod of earth with hie spade, and reversed it again with leisurely exertion of strength, seemed to wish he could as easily bury the young gentlemen beside him out of sight as he did the crumbling mould beneath him. The young gentlemen in question looked awfully demure whenever Lovell's eye glanced towards them, but exhibited the next moment an air of joyous impertinence, which boded ill for the aged gardener's peace of mind. The coachman, as he drove by, touched his hat to Lovell, and directly after pulled up, and, stepping down from the gig, ran back to the parsonage, and, again touching his hat, informed Lovell that—" Master was taken very bad."

Lovell left the gardener in the hands of the boys, and, opening the garden gate, joined the coachman outside. "What is the matter with him, John?" John shook his head, and intimated that it was a bad job. That master had had an " apoplexy." That he ought to be blooded. That John's grandfather went off in just such a fit. That he was a kind master to him, though he knew no more of a horse than a babe unborn. Lovell told the coachman that he should like to call at the house, and see if he could be of any service. This step was precisely what John intended should be taken, and he helped Lovell into the gig with great satisfaction, observing as he reassumed the reins, and gave Mr. Grierson's bony horse an impressive hint with the whip, that he for his part liked to see the parson treading on the doctor's heels.

"I'm afraid, John," said Lovell, "the Christian priest is often called in when it is too late."

" The parson, you mean, sir?" answered John. " Why, I'm afeard on't, sir. Look ye here, sir, if my master had a mind for one of his horses to run a race (which, poor gentleman! he would as soon run a race himself as even hear on), that 'ere horse had need be trained, and sweated, and exercised, and got in condition weeks afore the race come off. I'm of opinion, if it warn't so, he'd cut a sorry figure as he hobbled past the judge's stand." "Well, John, that's true enough; but we must never despair, however late we begin." . On arriving at Beaumont-house, Lovell found that tranquillity was in some measure restored. Mr. Grierson was still with his patient, who exhibited signs of returning consciousness. There was fair hope of restoration to comparative, if not to complete health. Perfect composure, and freedom from all exciting influences, were indispensable conditions of recovery. Lady Maud already felt her heart lighter. She, however, received Lovell's visit with thankfulness, and listened with some attention to the few words of a serious character he contrived to utter, during the five minutes she remained with him in the drawing-room. She left him in haste, with a little nervousness of manner, alleging as a reason that she might be wanted in the sick-room. Gertrude and the two girls were lying down in the school-room. As Lovell crossed the hall on his way out he lighted upon Mr. Grierson, drinking a glass of home-brewed beer with an air of enjoyment pleasant to behold. Let not the reader think Grierson in the smallest degree self-indulgent or intemperate for so doing. It was now four o'clock, and he had tasted nothing since his breakfast at eight o'clock, consisting of a cup of smoked coffee and a dubious egg, with a piece of bread which he put into the box seat of his gig intending to finish, but had forgotten to do so. He now had no time to partake of substantial food, but accepted a glass of beer to support him in his visits to two paupers eight miles asunder, to whom he was supplying sarsaparilla and quinine at the yearly rate of about a quarter of his salary, "By the bye, Lovell," said Mr. Grierson, "have yon heard the news from over the hills ? Sad riots!"

" Why," said Lovell, " I saw two or three yeomanry trotting to and fro this afternoon. I thought they were going to meet for drill or exercise."

" Not a bit of it! The navvies are burning Rent-worth, and the miners are marching to join them! They say poor Rubbley went down on his knees to the lord-lieutenant to ask for protection!"

" The navigators are not generally ill disposed," said Lovell. "What has put them out?"

" Much the same thing, I suspect, as put our poor friend up-stairs out," rejoined Grierson—" the railway break-down and panic. The men are gone wild. However, I must be off. I hope things will mend."

" Had I better stay a little longer ?"

"It would be as well," replied Grierson. "I shall look in again when I have ridden my sixteen miles. John must give my horse a mash. Well, I really do hope things will mend."

And, so saying, Mr. Grierson smiled hopefully at the butler who took his glass, then at Lovely then at John who was standing beside his gig at the front door, and lastly at his horse who seemed to feel the cheering influence, and set off without hesitation at the rate of nine miles an hour.

In the meanwhile, our Mend Miss Beverley had taken an unusually long excursion. She had walked to pay a visit to the governess of Colonel Clair's children, with whom she had of late been wont to confer at intervals on mutual grievances, as well as on the general degradation of their class. On the present occasion, the little Clairs being absent on a visit, Mrs. Clair invited Miss Beverley to take an early dinner with her friend. Accordingly the two governesses, Miss Beverley and Miss Seton, sat down to a very enjoyable repast of cutlets and curry, together with a bottle of excellent port. The colonel, being proud of his port, made the butler decant it in his presence, and then dogged him down the passage until he saw it safe inside the school-room. After a glass or two of this animating beverage, the ladies became communicative as well as sentimental. They marvelled at the early development of infant malignity. They discussed the particular merits and de-merits of their pupils. From thence they glanced casually to the flavour and quality of the last home-brewed beer; touched lightly upon the uncertain character of school-room tea; and glided into a short dissertation on the arrogance and pertness of ladies' maids and upper housemaids. Then Miss Seton, in confidence, informed Miss Beverley, that there was one intolerable and galling grievance which loaded her with moral fetters, and would certainly end in obliging her to seek a more genial sphere- This was, that Mrs. Clair frequently remitted or modified the punishments Miss Seton inflicted unwillingly, and as a solemn duty, upon the little Clairs.

" For instance," said Miss Seton; " the other day I was compelled to punish Fanny. She came to her music lesson with one thumb nail dirty. I ordered her to go to bed at six o'clock as a slight correction. Would you believe it? Mrs. Clair commuted the punishment to rising next morning an hour earlier than usual, alleging as a reason that it was Colonel Clair's birthday, and he liked to have his children about him! Festivity, and folly, and parental levity elevated above the duty we owe to a child's opening mind and budding offensiveness! It ties my hands and wrings my heart!"

And Miss Seton took a good sip of port wine as she completed her sentence. Then Miss Beverley began to intimate, that for her part she was sorry to say Lady Maud sometimes did not treat her with that delicate tact and generosity a lonely woman, intrusted with a great charge, might look for at her hands.

"For instance," proceeded Miss Beverley, "the onus of punishing my pupils is constantly deputed to *me*. It is mamma who is to kiss, and to praise, and pet them, *I* am to punish, scold, pull them this way and that. One day Lady Maud came to me and said, just bending her graceful neck round the corner of the school-room door: ' Miss Beverley, I am sorry to say Jessie and Agatha lay awake talking last night till nearly twelve o'clock. I should like you to give them a punishment.' Then I have to execute the disagreeable task of scolding them for half an hour, and giving them the verb *Dormir* to write out six times. It does chill one's best energies to be allotted only the drudgery and bitterness of education, while the mother engrosses the pleasantness and the interest of it. One soon wearies of inflicting punishment !"

"Do you?" interrupted Miss Seton. "Oh! but the duty of it! That is what keeps one up—the sense of duty! You see the passionate girl; the pert, malignant pupil; the dirty slut. A voice says—'Do your duty!' loudly in both ears. You punish. The conscience is satisfied— the child benefited'

Miss Seton waved a rather powerful hand so earnestly in the air as she said this, that Miss Beverley naturally asked, "Do you slap?"

" Sometimes. But I find a slight pinch apparently given in jest very effective. Don't you pinch ?"

" Oh! indeed, no!" answered Miss Beverley.

" Nor slap ? " inquired Miss Seton, in surprise.

" No!" cried Miss Beverley. " I don't mean to say I have never done such a thing in my life; but only when unusually provoked."

"My dear,' said Miss Seton, "you surprise me! Don't you even fillip ?"

" Why," answered Miss Beverley, blushing, " I con-fess I have at music; but very rarely."

"Well, your children are out of the common, I suppose."

"Pretty well. I am very fond of them after all. And then mammas are so jealous of the honour and luxury of striking their own flesh and blood. My poor friend Araminta Tarantula Smith"

" What a fine name!" said Miss Seton.

" Oh, you know, she was given those fine names in order to get her into the Governess' Institution. Sub-scribers generally vote in favour of the candidate who has the prettiest name. Well, Araminta Tarantula was governess to Mrs. Lahoope. The little Lahoopes were tiresome. She gave a mild box on the ear to each of the three in succession."

"Which I lave no doubt," observed Miss Seton, " they richly deserved."

"The children, like sad little telltales, told Mrs. Lahoope. In came Mrs. La-hoope—'Miss! if you dare touch my children, I tell you what, you shall never darken my doors again, Miss!' "

" What a mother!" exclaimed Miss Seaton. " One marvels whether the idiot or the tyrant is most conspicuous in her conduct!"

" However," continued Miss Beverley, " it all ended in hysterics and mulled wine; and they made it up again. But Araminta Tarantula for the future kept her fingers to herself, and I think she was right."

At this point of the conversation, word was sent up that the groom, who had ridden over to let Lady Maud know Miss Beverley was going to stay dinner, had brought back intelligence that Mr. Usherwood had had an apoplectic stroke, and was lying very ill.

Miss Beverley was rather shocked. She thought of the alarm and anguish of Lady Maud, of Gertrude, of the younger girls; and felt abashed to think she had been spending so much time in lamenting over trials and vexations of comparative unimportance. She did not like to cry before the strong-minded Miss Seton, but had a hard struggle to prevent it. " The Voice from the School-room" was in her pocket, meant for Miss Seton's perusal; but she altered her mind, and kept it where it was. Then took a hasty leave, and started over the hill for Beaumont-house,

CHAPTER X.

THE RIOTERS CROSS THE MOOR.

IT was late in the afternoon when strange rumours began to float about the neighbourhood, that a multitude of riotous men were pouring along the road, and across the fields extending between Okenham and the Bent-worth hills.

Now, to the west of Beaumont-house, that picturesque valley opened which we have already described to the reader as having apparently been at some time or other the channel of a huge river, or arm of the sea. The Manor-house Farm was situate on the side of the valley furthest from Beaumont-house, and could be distinctly seen from the plains beyond. An observer, on scaling the high ground at the back of the latter mansion, could obtain an extensive view of the country stretching. towards the Rentworth hills. It was for the most part a level plain intersected by straight roads and stagnant ditches, occasionally clothed, and that scantily, with groups of alder and ash; whilst here and there the eye detected a row of lean hungry-looking poplars, ranged along the distant road-side like a regiment of notes of admiration; or now and then an oak or two of sturdy but stunted proportions, rose flat as a mushroom out of that chilly soil. At long intervals dirty-white cottages lined the side of the road, with strips of garden ground in front of them raised in high ridges to let the wet run off: or a farm with its collection of irregular buildings grouped round it, sheltered by thickly planted trees: or an orchard, whose towering thorn-fence protected the moss-grown sickly-looking fruit-trees from the bleak winds that so often scoured the miles of damp black moor on either side. Taken alone, the level plain might have struck the eye as monotonous and dreary, but the fertile dopes leading up to the well-wooded hills on the north, cleft asunder by the steep gorge before alluded to, and occasionally near their summit breaking into masses of precipitous rocks; the long line of purple mountains which rose hazy in the distance beyond Rentworth, and formed the southern boundary of the moor; the glimpses of the tranquil sea, appearing here and there above the trees, for away to the west—altogether formed a landscape rich and interesting, full of novelty, replete with pleasing contrasts, upon which the spectator was not soon tired of gazing.

It was, then, amongst the hamlets scattered over the northern portion of this district, that the rumours above referred to began to gain ground. News of this kind travels fast; and, though the mob suffered no one to precede them, turning back or forcibly detaining every horseman, or spring-cart, or farmers coburgh that overtook them on the road; yet, whilst they were still distant from Beaumont-house five or six miles, the knowledge of their approach was spreading consternation through the district. It was said that several thousand desperate men were sweeping across the moor, destroying and trampling down the heavy crops that in favourable seasons rose from that rich alluvial land, pillaging orchards, tearing down fences, and levying contributions in the shape of cider, beer, and bread and cheese, on every farm-house they passed. This version of the number of the mob, and the devastations they were committing, was slightly exaggerated. When the rioters, re-assembling near the mines after their hasty re-treat from Rentworth, started for the moor, they certainly mustered near a thousand men, but this amount began to diminish before they had completed many miles of their journey Some thought better of it and tamed back, others were tired and lay down; some, again, turned into beer-shops and public-houses, and could not be got to stir out again. So that, by the time the rioters were about four miles from the place of their destination, they were but three or four hundred in number. Even these would probably have dwindled away still farther; but Harrill, who was now their chief leader, led them upon a farm-house near the road-side, and compelled the mistress to give them all the cider on her premises. This revived their drooping courage, and they once more started forwards, some running, some shouting, some singing, some brandishing various weapons of offence—such as fowling-pieces, old muskets, iron bars, pick-axes, and other tools used by navvies and miners, as well as pokers, reaping-hooks, and bludgeons. Resistance was not much thought of at Okenham, or any where else. In the first place, the principal farmers and gentlemen were in the yeomanry, and consequently far away. In the next place, it was believed that the multitude approaching were as has been said some thousands in number, and well armed. Many of the villagers fled, others hid themselves. As, however, it became more and more probable towards which point the mob were moving, people began to drop in one after the other at the back-door of Beaumont-house, to give notice of the approaching danger, and to tender advice or offer assistance as the case might be. Now it was the surgeon's positive injunction that the most absolute tranquillity should be preserved, not only in Mr. Usherwood's bedroom, but throughout the whole house. What was to be done !

This was a question nobody seemed able to solve. A hurried and agitated debate was held in the servants' hall. The extreme anxiety and perplexity of the emergency levelled all distinctions. Mrs. Millet, the housekeeper, forgot herself so far as to sit down upon an ordinary bench, instead of the broad-bottomed arm-chair which formed her usual throne, in a state of blank imbecility, quite stunned by the magnitude of the danger. Placing her hands on her knees, she incessantly asked, " Will any body tell us what we are to do?" repeating it over and over again without stopping, and looking straight into the fireplace all the time. By her side sat the kitchen-maid, who was sobbing and crying as if her heart would break, her face all smeared with tears and soot, having rubbed it with her hands just after cleaning a saucepan. The butler was giving one of the housemaids, who had been threatened with a faint, a wine-glass of choice Maraschino. The other housemaid was loud in talk with the page and footman, who, having differed as to the probable number of the mob, were only prevented from proceeding to blows by her vigorous interference. Three or four labouring men were drinking beer in another corner of the room, assisted by the coachman and two of the gardeners, Lucy Weston had been upstairs, but, on passing one of the back-doors of the mansion, she beheld her brother peering in as if in search for some one.

"George, what are you doing there? Come in directly," she said.

"Don't you know the news ?" he asked.

" To be sure. Every body is talking of it. What to do I don't "know. I daren't tell my young lady. If the old gentleman hiears it, he will go off at once."

"Well, Lucy, I've just stepped up to comfort you all'

" George dear, I'm afraid you can't help us," said Lucy despondingly.

" I tell you what," said Weston; " these fellows from Rentworth and the mines are under my thumb. Why, my dear little Lucy, don't you know I've lectured to them scores of times ? They owe me much. I opened their minds and told them all their grievances."

" Well, I know you're very clever, George," answered Lucy. "But they're a wild set. Will they mind you!"

" Mind me! I've drawn tears from their eyes in de-scribing to them their wretch-ed condition. One night I worked them up to such a pitch, that a whole lot of them sprang from their seats, and swore they would smash the aristocracy at a blow!"

Lucy, who was a pretty-looking girl with soft blue eyes, gazed at her brother admiringly, and, seizing his arm, cried, " Go then, dear George, stop them. Tell them this is a sad sick house—tell them"

"My poor child," interrupted Weston, "I know what to tell them. Make your-self easy. I shall bring them up as short as if they had come against a stone wall." "That's a good dear George," said Lucy. "And how smart you are too!" she added, noticing that he was dressed in his Sunday clothes—that is to say, a suit of, black with white cravat and waistcoat.

" Of course! 'This my lecturing dress. I think all uniform, livery, or costume of any sort—whether in king, parson, soldier or lawyer—a base mockery. But you see, Lucy, they wouldn't know me in my working-dress. And, Lucy, dear, just get me a glass of wine or something. I shall have to speak pretty loud, and strong too, perhaps."

Lucy ran off to the servants' hall, and announced publicly that her brother was going to lecture the mob, and send them all home; at the same time signifying her brother's request to the butler. That worthy, with the greatest alacrity, fetched a bottle of his master's choicest port, whilst the other servants trooped out of the hall and gathered reverentially round Weston, whom, a few hours before, they would have shrunk from 'with disgust. Mrs. Millet, however, still remained seated on the bench, exclaiming, though nobody was in the room—" Will any body tell me what to do ? "

In the butler's pantry the coachman had, however, collected a sort of opposi-tion party, consisting of two gardeners and the groom. These were employed in cleaning and loading two or three guns, a blunderbuss, and some pistols; whilst the under-housemaids, aided by the footman and page, employed themselves in shut-ting the outside Venetian blinds, and fastening the shutters of the lower windows.

Weston, after drinking his wine, hastened back towards the main road where a friendly baker was waiting for him in a coburgh cart. The baker had promised to give him a lift for a mile or two, so as to stop the progress of the mob as soon as possible. Having been driven about two miles, Weston desired him to pull up, for he could discern in the distance some of the more advanced portion of the mob pressing forwards along the road; first one or two—then in greater numbers. The foremost bore a banner, consisting of a sheet upon a barber's pole, bearing the inscription on one side of "Peace and Fraternity!" on the other, "A bellyful for us, or a bloody grave for you!" Another man close behind carried a flag, on which " Death to the Railway Rogues " was inscribed, with a skull and cross-bones coarsely painted under it; and above it, a heart stuck through with a butcher's knife. This flag was bespattered with blood; probably, that of a sheep or bullock.

Long before Weston had accurately made out these cheerful and inspiriting devices and inscriptions, the worthy baker had hastily bade him good-bye, and with an earnest request that he would mind what he was about and take care of himself, whipped his horse to a gallop and rattled his spring-cart back to Okenham. Here he aggravated the prevailing alarm by a vivid report of the frightful appearance of the savage horde trooping across the moor.

Weston stepped a little to one side of the road, and reconnoitred the disorderly procession as it neared the spot where he stood. Several fellows with smutted faces immediately followed the banner just described. These were walking in some sort of order, and had an air of ugly determination about them which Weston did not like, particularly as they had two or three guns amongst them, and bore heavy bludgeons on their shoulders. Behind them came a long straggling crowd of men and boys. Some walking arm-in-arm; some making rude music by beating iron pots with tongs and pokers; some clashing their sticks and weapons together, and yelling in chorus. A good many had jumped the ditches on either side, and were pursuing their course along the fields in a parallel line with those in the road. A few lagged behind or lay down to rest, either overcome with liquor or with fatigue.

The spectacle was not exactly a pleasant one, and the weekly lecturer at the Philanthropic Institute felt a momentary misgiving. But to escape was not easy, for there were ditches on each side, and the mob were in the fields as well as in the road. As they approached, he stopped and took off his hat. This salutation was returned by a decayed turnip flung at his head from the adjacent field. This was not encouraging; but stepping upon the trunk of a large oak-tree, recently felled, which lay along the side of the road, he held out his hand and claimed attention. " Why! blessed if it ain't our leeturer!" shouted a man who wore a tin saucepan on his head by way of a helmet. " It's orator Weston !" cried another, leaping on the tree trunk and slapping him on the back. " Hurrah I here's the doctor! Three cheers for Doctor Weston!" The mob, who were now beginning to stop and gather round the tree, shouted frantically, but only a few knew what it was all about. Presently, Harrill came running up, and recognizing Weston, cried out to him with an oath—

" What brings you here, you cursed fool ? What are you up to? Eh, you fool— eh? Don't you know there's no time to lose ! "

" My dear friends,' shouted Weston, not heeding the interruption—" my dear friends, it does my heart good to see you. This is a glorious triumph! Yes, gentle-men—yes, my dear friends, this is a great triumph, and I rejoice to witness it. May the great ones of the earth, Jongs, princes, peers, and parsons, take the lesson home to their corrupt hearts! May the besotted squire and the bloated bishop, may the mincing lady with *hex* painted face, may the whole herd of land-owners, house-owners, and mill-owners, parliament lords and cotton lords, roll and wriggle under your feet, a mass of festering corruption, never to rise again ! " Immense applause followed this exordium, and Weston proceeded with increased confidence. " My brave fellows, you are a lot of thorough-bred Britons, and no mistake ! I see before me many a village Hampden, and hear the voice of many a mute inglorious Mil-ton."

" George, thou cursed fool," interposed Harrill, " cut it short, I say!" And he griped his leg with an energy which brought tears to the orator's eyes.

" Gentlemen," resumed Weston, " tears rush to these horny eyes to behold this beautiful, this touching spectacle! The dumb suffering millions have indeed found a voice! Let it be heard! Roar into the ears of your oppressors those withering truths which to be acknowledged and obeyed need only to be heard! Roar, shout, proclaim to Europe, to the four quarters of the globe, that the people must have their rights ! But remember" Here the orator endeavoured to assume a solemn and impressive tone. "Remember, you must triumph by moral force. The calm force of reason and morality. The mild gushing radiance of truth gently yet irresistibly sweeping the shades of ignorance and error from a weary world. No brute violence. No drop of brother's blood. Oh, we must win them by love!" (exclaimed Weston, extending his arms wide, as if he wished to embrace all human kind at once—" by love— peace and love, instead of war and hatred!"

The mob by this time began to show signs of impatience, and the man with the tin pot on his head disrespectfully called out, " I say, old boy, your getting prosy!"

An ill-looking lad near him began to imitate Punch, to the extreme amusement of the multitude, whilst a stout fellow, with one of the balusters of the inn staircase in his hand, expressed a strong opinion that that 'ere rot might go down very well at the " Fill-and-sloppit Club," but " warn't of no account where there was any business afoot." Harrill roared to the men to push on, and waste no more time. But just at that moment a clod of earth, flung by some one in the adjacent field, hit Weston a smart blow on the shoulder. He turned with angry haste to see who had struck him, but, at the instant, slip went his foot, and over he went with his heels in the air towards the edge of the ditch. He tried to save himself, but the ground was slippery, and, in the twinkling of an eye, he shot plump into the ditch. A hoarse roar of merri-ment greeted this misadventure, and no one at first seemed disposed to aid the weekly lecturer at the Philanthropic Club, who emerged completely drenched in slimy black mud, and stood in the middle of the ditch up to his waist panting for breath. Harrill, however, and one or two others, presently gave him a hand, and he was rescued from his unpleasant position.

" Come along with us, doctor; never heed the filth! It's all the better, for thou wast rigged too much like a gemman afore!" exclaimed the man in the helmet. Whilst several of the mob seized hold of him, and, despite his struggles, hoisted him on their shoulders, shouting "The Doctor! The Doctor! Make way for the Doctor ! He's the man who'll physic the railway rogues!" Then hurrying along after the main body of their companions, carried Weston with them lifted up on high, angrily endeavouring to escape the honour conferred upon him.

On arriving at a point where four roads met, the mob again halted. They were now close to the hills of Oken-ham, and could just see the chimneys of Beaumont-house rising above the distant trees. To the left of the park and plantations, the entrance of the valley was seen to expand, richly wooded, and studded with cottages. Two or three grey church towers rose quietly among trees and cottages at intervals along the receding hills. Harrill waited until the stragglers and more erratic of the mob had joined the main body, and then, standing in the middle of his rough companions, proposed that himself, and a portion of the most active of the men, should turn off to the Manor Farm, and fire the ricks in the stack-yard. They had ascertained from several sources that Nugent's yeomanry troop had been called out, and had started that afternoon for Rentworth. Harrill therefore calculated upon haying this troop, and perhaps a detachment of infantry into the bargain, sooner or later at their heels.

The rioters had got out of the town, and started for the moor, making a slight detour towards the mines in order to deceive the military, three-quarters of an hour before the first detachment of troops entered Bent-worth. They were, therefore, considerably in advance of Nugent and his troop. Nevertheless, they were on foot, and well knew that every minute must lessen the distance between them and their mounted pursuers. Harrill therefore calculated upon drawing off the attention of the yeomanry, and especially of Nugent, from the real object of the mob's animosity which was Beau-mont-house, by setting the Manor Farm ricks and hay mows in a blaze. He judged the yeomanry would at once decide that the whole mob were ravaging the farm, and so turn off in that direction the moment they beheld so great a conflagration in the distance. Leaving the navvie in the helmet to lead on the bulk of the mul-titude, about two hundred in number, Harrill therefore went off with forty or fifty fellows along the road which led direct to the Manor Farm.

The mob were to proceed more leisurely in order to give time to Harrill to rejoin them, which he hoped to do in three-quarters of an hour by pushing across the country by a short cut from the Manor Farm. Weston was still carried along with the throng of men, some of whom were half drunk, and all in a reckless and desperate mood. Amidst the clamour and shouting, he could not get a hearing, but was only greeted with yells of "The Doctor for ever! " and clasped in the unsavoury embraces of those nearest to him. He could not easily extricate himself from such a disorderly procession except at the risk of being flung down, or of falling again into the ditch. He was now on his legs, but his companions occasionally took his arm on either side, and dragged him along between them.

As, however, they neared the village of Okenham, the foremost of the multitude seemed to slacken their pace, and the banner with the skull and cross-bones fell gradually to the rear. The chief leaders were in loud altercation as to what was to be done when they reached Beaumont-house. Drink was the first thing desired by the tired and thirsty mob. Some, however, were cool-headed enough to determine that a good purseful of gold, or, In default of gold, plenty of solid silver plate, should be handed out by old Usherwood, or they would have his house about his ears. A few had more desperate designs in view. They meditated a regular assault upon, the mansion, and anticipated plundering and ravaging it from top to bottom. A large number, however, were of quite a different stamp, and had no malicious object in view; nay, would have shrunk from any deliberate act of cruelty or dishonesty. All they Intended was to make a demonstration to frighten the railway directors whom they regarded as downright thieves, into doing justice by those in their employ.

For it is rare that outbreaks of this kind take place without strong provocation, and often and often the chief culprits are those who have goaded the working classes by repeated acts of injustice or cruelty into a state of frenzy that disables them from knowing right from wrong, and lays them open to the influence of selfish and designing men.

At this juncture Weston took the opportunity, unobserved, to escape across an adjoining field, nor did he stop running until he had put a considerable distance between himself and the riotous assemblage in the Kent-worth road. He paused at last, however, and looked about him, as if to make sure of his whereabouts.

" Ah! there is the lane leading to Eastwood two fields off. I know it by the crooked pollard ash. Then beyond is the hill which stretches away towards Claw-thorp. Clawthorp," he repeated—" Clawthorp, and at Claw-thorp is the lunatic asylum. Would I had never seen it! But all is over now. She is dead—dead, and buried! And I am here—wretched and despised—dogged and persecuted by Har-rill—obliged to submit, yet loathing him from the bottom of my soul. If it were not for Lucy, I could envy that poor lady, first smitten by madness then passing from madness to death! But I must live to watch over and comfort Lucy, come what will. Even if I am disgraced, we can fly to Australia— that is, if she would but get stronger—would but get stronger. But I must not waste time. I must try to thwart that scoundrel Harrill Fool that I was, to think that my gibberish could influence that mob! Upon my word, I have had a bit of a lesson! " And he gazed ruefully at his muddy and dripping garments. " I must \ run, if it is but to keep myself warm. Let me see. There is Colonel Clair. He is a good plucky fellow. The yeomanry will be up before nightfall, that's sure. All we want is to gain time. I'll cross the river by the mill-dam, and be over to Colonel Clair's in no time. I think hell help us. But if Harrill hears of it, I am as good as ruined. Well, I'll risk it. So here goes !"

And Weston pushed forwards across the fields in the direction of Eastwood Lane.

We must now, however, return to Beaumont-house. Here, as we have stated, every thing was in commotion. Miss Beverley had just returned, and, finding no one would undertake the task of communicating to Lady Maud the alarming intelligence from Rentworth, determined to undertake this unpleasant duty herself, and had run up-stairs accordingly. The clatter of tongues and general disturbance was of course mostly confined to the servants' part of the house, and Lovell had been quietly sitting in the drawing-room, reading a new Quarterly, that contained an ecclesiastical article painfully interesting to him, in blissful ignorance of the excitement prevailing in the household. At length, however, the servants, who, we have said, were busy closing shutters and outside blinds, reached the drawing-room windows, and, standing on the lawn outside, commenced closing the jalousies or outside shutters, ignorant that any one was sitting in the room. They did so gently, for fear of disturbing the sick gentleman above, and Lovell heard them not; but the room, as each shutter was closed, becoming darker and darker, he began to conclude that night was setting In fast. So, closing his book, he rose from his chair, and suddenly perceived what the servants were about. On asking what was the matter they breathlessly told him, both speaking together, the news of the approach of the rioters, just brought to the house. At that moment Lady Maud rushed down-stairs followed by Miss Beverley, and Lovell heard her addressing the servants in the hall in a voice tremulous with emotion. He hastened in the same direction, and was met by Lady Maud at the doorway in a state of the deepest anxiety and distress.

"Mr. Lovell, dear sir, can you help us? Is there any thing to be done ? Can you advise us ? "

"How many are the rioters, and whereabouts are they ? " asked Lovell

"They must be within three miles of us—there are hundreds of them—some say thousands —and they are bound for this house! There is no doubt ofit!"

" But are you sure, Lady Maud—are you sure ? "

" Yes, yes, yes—every body says so. There is no doubt of it. My poor husband's connection with the Railway has exposed him to the hatred of the rioters. They think that he, poor man, is one of those who have injured them, whereas he is a fellow-victim with themselves."

" How many men have you on the premises ? " Lovell went on to inquire hastily; " and what arms have you ? A few resolute fellows, well armed, can keep hundreds at bay."

" Arms ? men ?" cried Lady Maud." The first shot fired will be death to my husband. Perfect quiet is the sole means of saving his life. If the mob merely stand and shout without lifting a little finger against the house, it is enough—it will do—it will kill him—kill him, Mr. Lovell!" she said. seizing his arm firmly.

Lovell was indeed staggered.

"Have you spread the alarm? Have you sent to Okenham?"

" People have been sent in various directions. We expect the yeomanry before night. It is our sole hope."

Lady Maud walked to and fro hastily, and without that soft leisurely grace usually visible in her movements. She was no longer a fine lady gliding swan-like through the shallows of fashionable life. She was an anxious, grief-stricken woman, struggling with danger and calamity. She clenched her little hand with energy, and exclaimed—

"If I were a man, I would meet those fellows face to face in the high-road, and tell them the plain facts of the case. Then, if they still persisted, I would shoot the foremost dead, and let the rest kill me and all I love afterwardsI"

"Lady Maud," said Lovell taking her hand, "be calm. I will do my best to help you. Be calm, and trust in God."

" His wrath is gone out against me," replied Lady Maud, bitterly.

"But in wrath he remembers mercy. He desires to draw you to him. Submit to his will in faith. Seek him, Lady Maud, in prayer. Meanwhile, I will do my best to save those you love from injury."

Lady Maud pressed his hand almost with a feeling of affection, and retained it for a moment. But it was a time for action; and Lovell, after another word or two of encouragement, and without listening to his companion's expressions of anxiety about his personal safety, hastened from the room, and desired two or three of the men-servants and others about the place upon whom he thought he could depend, to meet him on the lawn in front of the house. He himself went thither immediately, and, standing upon the higher ground, carefully and thoughtfully — yet as rapidly as he could—surveyed the country immediately in front of Beaumont-house, between the park and the wide marshy plain of which we have already spoken.

CHAPTER XL

DEFENCE OF BEAUMONT-HOUSE,

ABOUT a couple of hundred yards from the lodge leading into the park of Beaumont-house, wound a small stream along the valley slowly and sluggishly except when swelled by autumn rains or by winter snow; for at such times it was both rapid and deep, dangerous indeed even for a good swimmer to attempt to ford. Now, the main road from Rentworth crossed this stream by means of a small narrow bridge, and it immediately struck Lovell, that if the mob were advancing towards Beaumont-house along this road, here was the point at which a stand should be made; for ex-cept at this bridge there was no possibility of crossing the stream for nearly a quarter of a mile on either side, and even at those points the means of transit was a simple plank of rough elm, which a couple of men could displace and draw over to the Beaumont side of the river. There had been, it should be premised, much rain during the last fortnight, and the river rushed brimming full between its steep and slippery bank, affording an effectual barrier to man or beast who should attempt to ford it.

Without wasting much time in consultation—for time was precious—Lovell, whose plan was at once and warmly approved by John and one or two of the bettermost class of labourers about the premises, immediately collected all the able-bodied men he could find in the immediate vicinity of the house, and gave them their instructions as clearly and emphatically as he could.

The Reverend Augustine Smithers, late fellow of Oriel, would have been rather amazed to see with what promptitude and good sense, Lovell, now left to his own resources, or as it is called his own " mother wit," dealt with the difficulties confronting him. The Reverend Augustine Smithers, we say, would have been amazed, and, we are strongly inclined to believe, would have found out that his fancied superiority to Lovell was a delusion, and the sooner it was dissipated the better would it be for both of them.

Lovell had noticed in the wood-yard behind Beaumont-house a waggon of fresh cut thorns, brought in for the purpose of stopping certain gaps in the park fence, which had not yet, in consequence of the damp weather, been hauled out into the park. This wagon Lovell desired John to harness his horses to, and haul to the little bridge of which we have just spoken. He himself at once started for the bridge accompanied by a dozen or more labourers, some of whom carried iron bars and pick-axes, whilst others were provided with stout ash sticks and strong stakes. Arriving at the bridge, Lovell's first care was to direct the men to heave a portion of the parapet into the river. Then, as soon as the waggon arrived, the thorns were pitched out in a large heap at the further end of the bridge, and propped up and fastened into a solid mass by stakes driven into the gound. The whole being further strengthened by a few lengths of wire for fencing purposes, twisted round and round it in every direction. The waggon was next drawn across the nearer end of the bridge and upset. Whilst against it was piled a quantity of turf recently cut from the roadside. This formed a pretty safe parapet to defend Lovell and his party not merely from lighter missiles, such as stones and pebbles, but from gun or pistol shot, should such be discharged at them.

It required half an hour's strenuous exertion to pre-pare this new species of barricade, but the men worked with a will. Lovell inspired them all with energy.

He Could not but doubt, as he noticed the eager promptitude with which the men about him caught at all he said, and comprehended the earnest straightforward words, whether of direction or of encouragement that he uttered from time to time—he could not but doubt whether the Reverend Augustine Smithers was quite right in urging him never to put much emotion into his sermon, nor seek to stimulate and rouse so much as to calmly edify and soberly instruct; keeping a level tone and a level style in harmony with the liturgy which he had just been intoning. " Certainly I want men to think about their souls—to turn away from sin, and to seek to serve God and their fellow-creatures, just as much as I want to induce these labourers to do the work we have now in hand. Certainly this is so. Therefore, why should I not speak right at my congregation. aim straight at them, just as I address the work-men round me?"

Lovell, highly satisfied with his essay in the art of extempore fortification, was just sending a messenger back to Beaumont-house to tell Lady Maud and the ladies to take heart, for he fully expected to keep the mob at bay until the yeomanry who could not be far off should come to their aid, when he heard the sound of a carriage passing rapidly along the high-road to Westerbourne, that crossed the Rentworth road at right angles on the Beaumont-house side of the bridge. Turning, he noticed that the carriage was Sir Eliot Prichard's. It stopped, and that worthy knight alighting, hastily came towards him, speaking rather out of breath.

" Beg your pardon, Mr. Lovell. Have heard strange stories as I passed the last turnpike in my way from Eastwood station. You know I've been in town for a few days. Only returned this morning. ' Find there have been riots—railway riots, and likely to be more—and likely to be more. So I am bound for home. Every magistrate you see should be at his post, Mr. Lovell—at his post where he can be found when wanted. But what in the world are you doing here, Mr. Lovell ? " The last question was uttered as he came close up to Lovell, and had a full view of the thorns and the parapet.

"The mob are coming this way," replied Lovell quietly. " They want to burn Usherwood's house be-cause he's a director, and we mean to stop them."

" Then I must be off home!" rejoined Sir Eliot with renewed energy. I must be at my post—at my post" where I can be found when wanted. I must be off home!" He paused as he was in the act of turning, and lowering his voice, added—" I'm extremely concerned to hear this about Usherwood."

" His illness ? Yes," rejoined Lovell.

"No, no, no! Illness is illness, and can't be helped. I mean his losses in this unfortunate line, Mr. Lovell— his losses! You have heard of them, of course ? "

Lovell hastily assented, for he began to think the knight was a dreadful bore at such a moment.

" You will see Lady Maud by and bye ? " continued . Sir Eliot.

" Perhaps I may."

" Then be so kind as to give her this little note, please. Many thanks, Mr. Lovell."

Lovell took the note, half-unconsciously, looking steadfastly down the Rentworth road, that at some distance off was on a sudden shrouded in a cloud of dust.

" Here they are!" cried Lovell.

" Here they are!" shouted the men.

" What, the rioters % " exclaimed Sir Eliot. " Then I must lose no time. I must be at my post—at my post where I can be found I Stand firm, Mr. Lovell—stand firm! If I meet the Westerbourne constable I will send him along to help you; but I fear being a baker he'll be detained, for to-day is baking day." And Sir Eliot sprang into his carriage and drove off home—" to his post!"

Lovell drew up his men and showed a bold front to the advancing rioters, who, shouting and yelling, came pressing onwards, a long straggling multitude waving their banners, now and then clashing their weapons together, now and then firing off a pistol or gun.

As they caught sight of the mansion, standing pleasantly on a slope of grassy lawn, with timber behind it and on either side, they seemed to gain redoubled vigour; and, closing up into a more compact body, advanced with less outward demonstration of mischief, but with plenty of desperate resolution in their hearts. No sooner, however, had they approached within a moderate distance of the bridge, which they evidently eyed with some misgiving and perplexity, than Lovell shouted to them— " Hold hard, or my men will fire !"

This menace, uttered in a clear determined voice, seemed to have a considerable effect. The multitude hung back, and the leaders commenced an animated conference. Lovell, considering this was a good moment for attempting a parley, now sprang up on the waggon, and asked to be heard for a few minutes.

There was a confused jabber of many voices in reply. Some one cried out "Halloo! Here's the parson!" Others shouted in tones of mock reverence, Silence !" Don't you see he's going to preach a sermon! " " Order, order!" cried several; "Where's the beadle?" "Fire away, parson!" "Take a pinch of snuff, your honour, afore you begin," asked a youth who squinted frightfully, throwing a handful of gravel at Lovell's head, which excited much applause, and a pretence of great indignation in the man with the tin pot on his head, who flung his helmet at the boy, shouting, " You desperate villain, how dare you insult his grace the archbishop ?" Amidst this confusion and noisy insolence, Lovell for a few moments vainly attempted to gain a hearing. He waited patiently, however, until the mob began to get tired, and the noise somewhat subsided. Then, taking advantage of a moment's pause, and in a loud voice he said, "Will you let me speak a very few words to you! Just hear me for a few minutes. That's all I ask." " Well," cried one or two, " go a-head then. Only cut it short!" Lovell managed to make himself heard. He spoke with so much earnestness, that the men were a little overawed and their attention awakened against their will.

"I don't know," said Lovell, "what you want here. You may have been very ill used. Of that I am no judge; but all I wish to tell you is this: The poor gentleman to whom that house belongs was taken ill this morning, and is lying on his back in danger of his life. His only chance of recovery is to be kept quiet. If you come shouting round the house: if you compel the armed men and servants to fire upon you, filling the place with tumult—you will kill the sick man, as surely as if you cut his throat!" The men shouted, "A good riddance, too! Ain't he a director? Hasn't he picked our pockets in cold blood, the scurvy old knave?"

"Believe me," cried Lovell—"believe me, he is more a loser from the Railroad Company than you are. I am told he is a ruined man. At all events if you attack the house he will be a murdered man. And what good will that do you, my friends? He has a wife and family as many of you have. Think of that now. You wouldn't hurt women and children—would you now, my men? I know you wouldn't."

" Parson, that's gammon!" interrupted the man with the helmet, who was afraid his companions might be softened by this appeal. "What cash have you got for us? Come, fork out!"

This was received with loud shouts of applause. Lovell could only assure them that Usherwood had lost thousands by the railway, and had no money tospare. But he would engage if they dispersed quietly, that Usher-wood, within twenty-four hours, should pay the sum of one hundred pounds into the hands of any one they chose to name, to be divided amongst the miners and navigators at Rentworth. And again he urged them to have compassion on the family, as well as on the sick man himself, assuring them they should not cross the bridge without a tough fightforit. Unfortunately the mob, many of whom were excited by liquor, knew that Harrill could not be far off. The black smoke from the burning ricks at the Manor-house Farm rose high in the air, and he was to make straight for Beaumont-house as soon as he had accomplished his purpose at the farm. This emboldened the more daring and mischievous spirits amongst them, and enabled them to over-ride the better feelings gaining ground amongst the bulk of the multi-tude. They knew that Har-rill, with his band of resolute followers, would speedily settle the question of cross-ing the bridge, and the rest was easy enough. Accordingly, they suddenly let fly a shower of stones at Lovell and his party. Whilst others creeping along the ditches on each side of the road, reconnoitred the strength of Lovell's position, and the number of his followers.

Apparently, the mob were reassured by the report given; for they commenced a methodical bombardment with stones and pebbles, seldom however hitting any of the defenders of the bridge; and two or three times firing off a musket at any one who exposed too much of his head and shoulders above the embankment of turf across the road. Although, therefore, no injury of any consequence was inflicted, there was quite enough risk incurred by Lovell's party to keep their attention alive. Emboldened by no firearms being discharged, the mob now at a given signal suddenly made a rush at the bridge. Lovell, to keep his word, fired the guns which he kept under his own control over the heads of the multitude. The only effect was to alarm the hindmost of them, who shrank back looking at each other to see if any one was hurt. This was not wholly without advantage to Lovell; for the consequence was that the front ranks of the mob were not driven on with the force and impetuosity resulting from pressure from behind, but came upon the fence opposed to them with only their own individual vigour.

Entangled amidst the thorns, with hands and feces scratched and lacerated, they had scarcely made any im-pression upon the barrier before them, when Lovell's men, springing over the turf and over the waggon, fell upon their assailants with the long ash staves with which Lovell had armed them, and, showering upon them a regular storm of blows, drove them, bruised and wounded, back towards the main body of the mob, who uttered a prolonged howl of rage and disappointment. Lovell's people had just retreated behind their turf embankment, when another kind of shout was raised by the mob, which Lovell did not like. It was a cry of savage delight and exultation. A moment after, seeing their countenances all turned in one direction, Lovell looked round and beheld, with no little anxiety and alarm, a number of men, evidently part of the rioters, hurrying along the road leading from Okenham valley, and, consequently, about to take Lovell's little intrenchment in the rear.

Now, it is a most uncomfortable sensation being taken in flank, or attacked in the rear, when you are already fully occupied with an enemy in your front. It tries the nerves of the bravest men; and it certainly sent dismay through the ranks of Lovell's small band of followers.

" For heaven's sake, load the guns, sir !" cried John. " And give 'em a dose of cold shot, or we are done for!"

The detachment of rioters in the rear was no other than Harrill and his party, who, having fired Nugent's ricks, were now hastening, as they supposed, to join in the plunder of Beaumont-house. These new-comers were still a couple of hundred yards off, and John's advice could scarcely be rejected with common prudence. But Lovell insisted in retaining charge of the guns, in order that no firing should take place except at the last extremity, as a matter of simple self-defence.

The mob on the further aide of the bridge rent the air with shouts that were ex-ultingly answered by tote thirty or forty men hastening towards the scene of action, headed by Harrill " They are too many for us!" exclaimed Lovell. " It will be useless waste of blood, attempting to hold the bridge longer. We must fall back upon the house, and try to make a stand at the entrance gate of the lawn."

Lovell's men had long before come to the same conelusion, and they started at a pretty sharp pace from the bridge towards a private door which led into the park, in a direction opposite to that Harrill was pursuing. The rioters on the other side of the bridge immediately made a rush at the thorns, but it was still no very pleasant matter to break their way through, and their very numbers impeded and embar-rassed them. Whilst at that moment the party headed by Harrill came to a dead stop about thirty yards from the lodge. Some of Lovell's men exclaimed—" Can it be the soldiers ? " No! the men were all staring at the lodge. What held them in check? Out of an open window protruded the long old-fashioned barrel of a gun, pointed in a menacing manner at the advancing detachment of rioters. Certainly, there was only one gun against thirty men, but then each of the men said to himself, "Shall I be the man shot?" Therefore, for a few seconds, every one faltered and hung back. But Har-rill cautiously approached the lodge-window, keeping to one side of the road, and then, making a rush, discovered it was merely old Andrew's rusty gun without a lock that had been propped up at the window by the owner previous to his prudent retreat some two hours before. On came the men with a yell, and broke at once through the lodge-gates into the park, whilst, about the same time, many of the mob at the bridge having forced their way through the thorns, ran, shouting wildly, in the same direction.

Lovell hastened with his party up the private path leading to the lawn gate, but his mind now misgave him. Unless he could parley again with the rioters, all was lost.

But just then, as the mob began to spread themselves over the park, directing their course towards the mansion that rose invitingly on the platform of lawn a few hundred yards distant—just then Lovell's small party were joined by an unexpected reinforcement, in the shape of Colonel Clair and about a dozen or so of active men, most of them his own servants, whom he had hastly collected. The Colonel and Lovell shook hands with the warmth that springs from a sense of common danger, and exchanged a few hurried words. It appeared that news of the rioters' approach had been brought to Colonel Clair by a man so covered with black mud from head to foot, that nobody could tell whether he was a stranger or a native of the place. Only he seemed very much in earnest., and the Colonel thought he would start with some men and reconnoitre. On the road ample corroboration was furnished of the truth of the statement, and the party hurried onwards with all speed.

As soon as the leaders of the mob perceived that the entrance gates of the lawn, as well as the sunk fence and low wall protecting it, were occupied by Lovell and Colonel Clair with a pretty strong party of men apparently armed, they were somewhat staggered, and gathering together as thick as bees near the lodge gates, held a brief conference to settle their plan of operations. They then suddenly broke into two divisions, one of which boldly advanced on the lawn gates and sunk fence, whilst the other diverged in an oblique direction, evidently for the purpose of at-tacking the back part of the premises.

The position of the defenders of the lawn now became rather unpleasant; and, to make the matter worse, two or three of the rioters carrying firearms, commenced coolly taking aim and firing at the wall and bushes behind which they were screening themselves. Still Lovell would not give up the firearms he had charge of, alleging it would only cause useless bloodshed, and that until the last extremity, when the house was actually attacked, they would not be justified in firing. Nevertheless, Colonel Clair's game-keeper, whose feelings suddenly carried him away, let fly his double-barrelled gun right amongst the more advanced of the rioters, and, wounding two or three of them about the legs, considerably checked the ardour of those in front. Still they gained ground, pushing on in scattered parties, whilst the other division of assailants rapidly neared the back part of Beaumont-house. It was time to fall back. Lovell and Colonel Clair both exclaimed simultaneously—

" The house I The house I Make for the house!" The whole party rose at once and made a rush for the house, whilst the shots fired by the rioters whizzed passed them, and fierce yells rang in their ears.

Harrill, maddened by liquor which he had procured as he came through the village, and brandishing a crow-bar, rushed forwards and burst through the lawn gates, followed by the most reckless of his companions.

At that instant a cry arose simultaneously from the house and from the rearmost of the rioters,—"The soldiers 1 the soldiers!"

All eyes were turned towards the Rentworth Road. Evening was far advanced; but the large masses of clouds in the eastern part of the sky, floating at a high elevation, gleamed white and silvery in the rays of the now descended sun, and shed a soft light over the broad plains beneath. Along the straight and level road could be seen a cloud of dust advancing, and every now and then the glitter of polished steel. As they gazed, they recognised more and more distinctly the dark forms of men and horses, and heard the sound of hoofs re-echoing like distant thunder along the hollow road.

A sudden panic seized the rioters. They fled in all directions. The park was strewed with flags, bludgeons, weapons of every description. Some of the men rushed towards the lodge gates, but many more ran for the park palings and scrambled over as well as they could; whilst others, more wary, made for the hill above Beaumont-house, hoping to escape amongst the woods and plantations. Harrill, enraged, would have made a stand even though the yeomanry were in sight, but his followers would not rally. They fled to right and left.

The party of servants and labourers, who with Colonel Clair and Lovell had been defending the entrance to the lawn, now sallied forth and endeavoured to evertake and capture some of the hindmost of the flying rioters. John who had seized up one of the fowling-pieces at the moment of the rush made by his party towards the house, set off in the direction of the park palings at a steady trot carrying the gun on his shoulder. As he crossed the drive he met Lovell, pale and without his hat, having been knocked down whilst making for the house by a stone flung from the mob, and slightly stunned. He had laid down, however, behind a clump of shrubs on the lawn for two or three minutes, and was tolerably himself again.

" John," he cried, " where are you off to?"

John, touching his hat, and dropping from a trot into a walk, answered—

" I'm just getting out of hearing of master, sir, so as not to disturb him, and then won't I have a pop at some of them rascals!" And he looked to see if the cap of his gun was all right.

" Nonsense, John; let them run! The sooner they are out of sight the better."

"I'll give 'em a fair start, sir. Won't shoot 'em standing, sir. Won't, indeed. Should like to mark one on 'em, sir!" he added, looking wistfully at the man who wore the tin-pot, but who had just flung it away and was trying to scale the palings, " Just one on 'em, sir!"

"Don't you mark your hands, Jóhn, with a fellow creature's blood. You will not feel the happier for it when the bustle is all over, I can tell you;" and Lovell took away the gun, and added, "Now look sharp, and get out the horses. We must clear the bridge. The yeomanry are brought to a stand-still. Get out the horses to haul away the waggon; and take some of the men along with you."

This was true enough, and so far was an advantage to the mob; very few of whom were in consequence taken prisoners. Harrill, we may as well mention, escaped over the hills; and, it was soon currently reported, had got clear away to S—shire, his native county. At all events, he eluded his pursuers, and, having taken refuge amongst his old haunts, all attempts to track him and apprehend him, proved ineffectual. We shall not again encounter Harrill, until, in an evil hour for him, he will again revisit the neighbourhood of the Manor-house Farm.

Meanwhile, as Lovell had anticipated, the yeomanry were brought up short by the substantial barricade at Okenham Bridge. The thorns had been mostly pitched into the river, and the stakes were easily removed; but it was not so easy to shift the waggon, jammed as it was between the parapets of the bridge, with a solid mass of turf piled against it. The yeomanry, however, dismounted, and being aided by John with a few of the labourers, soon cleared the passage, and then remounting, clattered along the road towards the lodge gates. Here they halted, and were despatched by Nugent in different directions in pursuit of the rioters. He himself, with one or two of his men, turned towards Beaumont-house, anxious to ascertain how matters fared there. About the same moment a messenger reached him from the Manor Farm, with the satisfactory intelligence that the fire was in a fair way of being got under, thanks to the wind having opportunely shifted. Whilst the men were at work clearing the bridge, Lovell remembered the note Sir Eliot Prichard had given him for Lady Maud, and walked up to the house as fast as the exhaustion and giddiness consequent on his hard day's work and the bruises he had received in the melée, permitted.

At Beaumont-house alarm and agony of mind had given place to gratitude and joy. Lady Maud, Ger-trude, all the inmates of the house, except the sick man who lay in drowsy half-consciousness in his luxurious bedchamber, had watched the gradual approach of the rioters ; their sudden check at the bridge which was visible from the upper windows; their parley with Lovell; their onslaught on the barricade and the successful defence of it by Lovell's party. After this, there had been some minutes' suspense, for Harrill's arrival on the scene could not be seen from the house. Only they had heard shouts and yells of seeming triumph and exultation.' Then the wild influx of the multitude into the park, spread a terrible panic through the household. Next came the stand made by Lovell aided by Colonel Clair and his men at the lawn gates and the sunk fence, the exciting scene that followed, and finally the long and ardently-desired appearance of the soldiery sweeping along the distant highway. With pale faces, grasping each others' hands, the women stood at different windows in the upper story of the house watching all that passed, but scarce uttering a word save hasty ejaculations of terror, surprise, or hope. No sooner had the yeomanry come fairly in sight, than there was a simultaneous cry of joy from all the assemblage. Some burst into tears. Some shook each other's hands for several minutes without stopping. Miss Beverley found herself embracing the under housemaid. Lady Maud hurried to her husband's room, followed by Gertrude, and, opening the door, exclaimed to the surgeon who was sitting by the sick man's side, " Saved! The yeomanry are in sight!" Mr. Grierson's face expanded into a perfectly pantomimic expression of hilarity. As for Mr. Usher-wood, the gradually-augmenting tumult did not appear to have yet reached his ear. He had merely murmured when an unusually loud shout or the distant report of a gun penetrated the closed shutters and curtains of the apartment, a few words about the train starting and the whistle of the engine, and on swallowing a dose of physic exclaimed somewhat authoritatively, " Pass the bottle !" Otherwise he had been tolerably composed and tranquil, and in Mr. Grierson's opinion was progressing favourably towards recovery. The mother and daughter then hastened to the schoolroom to see after Agatha and Jessie, who had been secluded there in a state of fear and trembling most of this eventful day. As for the rest of the household, they soon recovered their equanimity. Even Lucy Weston, who had been in great trouble about her brother, fearing that what with rioters, and what with yeomanry, he had come to some terrible end, was much reassured by the information that he had been recognised by some of Colonel Clair's people, covered indeed with mud, but otherwise quite safe and sound. Mrs. Paine, having passed several hours concealed under a four-post bed, emerged cautiously about midnight, with her dress in some disorder, and a smell-ing-bottle in each hand. Mrs. Millet, having recently risen from the bench where she had been sitting all day and was in consequence stiff about the limbs, moved about like a petrifaction partially reanimated, occasionally exclaiming with a vacant look, " Will any body tell me what I am to do ? " But by degrees recovering herself, proceeded with her work as usual.

Some anxiety was felt about old Andrew at the lodge, who had totally disap-peared and could nowhere be heard of. On the evening however of the following day, he was seen walking through the village with very dusty shoes on his way to the lodge, which he quietly re-entered, and commenced putting things to rights—first of all reverentially replacing his gun above the chimney-piece. . It was sur-mised by the most competent judges, that he had walked home to his friends some twelve miles off on the very first rumour of the rioters' approach.

At the entrance-hall Lovell was presently met by Lady Maud and Gertrude, and of course had to endure what to him was a particularly unpleasant process; namely, a passionate volley of thanks, interspersed with strong expressions of ad-mirationat his coolness, courage, etc., etc. Lovell turned red, held down his head, shuffled his feet to and fro, and, infact, looked like some one suddenly detected in an attempt at petty larceny, or other minor delinquency punishable by law. So, to extricate himself from the distress and embarrassment inflicted on him by the two ladies, he produced Sir Eliot Prichard's note with the rapidity of a government mes-senger delivering an express.

Lady Maud glanced at the direction, coloured slightly, opened the note, which was a thin sheet of cheap straw paper, and read as follows:—

" BURLINGTON HOTEL, LONDON.

" MY DEAR LADY MAUD,—

" Events have followed each other so rapidly since the day before yesterday, when I penned with much anxiety and a heart agitated by the tenderest emotions, the letter you have no doubt received embodying my sentiments towards your eldest daughter—that the mind grows confused and giddy as it looks back upon the past, and almost questions the fact of its own identity. The sad and runious ***boule-versement*** —I may say smash— of the North Rentworth Railway Company, has been a severe shock to mein many ways. It wounds me deeply to have to say it; but the pecuniary losses inflicted upon me by that catastrophe, must, I fear, put an impassable bar between me and the object of my tenderest ambition. I am not so selfish, Lady Maud, as to ask you to wed your daughter to a man whose income has been unfortunately reduced as mine has been. I, ***at once and without reservation,*** though with an ***aching heart,*** retract the offer I have made for your daughter's hand. May she be happy! May she be as happy as she ***deserves*** to be! ***More*** than this I cannot say.—I am, dear Lady Maud, most faithfully yours,

" ELIOT PRICHARD."

" P.S.—Excuse this very indifferent note-paper, but a man of shattered fortune must not be nice in his stationery ."

Lady Maud's handsome face, as she read these lines, gradually settled into an expression of loathing and contempt. Lovell and Gertrude had withdrawn a little, and she said to herself, as she folded up the note and placed it in her bosom,—

" This is a curiosity. I must take care of it. Shattered fortunes! The contemptible liar! Mr. Rubbley only the other day told me that Sir Eliot's investment in Rentworth railway stock amounted precisely to two thousand pounds! The plausible, mean-spirited but, nonsense—nonsense—this is silly !"

And Lady Maud with a smiling face turned to talk to Colonel Clair, and to beg him to take some refreshment in the dining-room, where a repast, consisting of tea and coffee, wine and beer, with plenty of cold meat, had been hastily laid out by the servants of the establishment.

" And take Mr, Lovell with you, Colonel," said Lady Maud; "lam sure he needs something."

" He's a fine fellow—a very brave active fellow, and deserves a medal!" exclaimed the Colonel, taking Lovell once more crimson with embarrassment by the arm, and carrying him off to the dining-room.

At that instant Nugent rode up to the front door covered with dust, and his horse drenched in white foam. Flinging the reins to one of the troopers who followed him, he dismounted and entered the well-known hall just as Gertrude and her mother were about to quit it. Gertrude blushed scarlet. As for Lady Maud she preserved her self-possession, advanced gracefully to Nugent, took both his hands in hers, and thanked him for the promptitude with which he had come to their aid, Nugent took these demonstrations tranquilly enough, and turned to speak to Gertrude, but she had fled from the room.

" Mr. Nugent," said Lady Maud, drawing him into the recess of a large bow window looking upon the lawn, " I know all that has passed between my daughter and yourself."

" I was on my way, Lady Maud, to your house this morning, meaning to explain every thing and put myself entirely in your hands, when a despatch reached me calling me to summon my troop, and push at once for Rentworth. I hope you believe that I meant to make no concealments. I know that I am by no means such a suitor as you might fairly expect for your daughter. I know that I am every way unworthy."

"Mr. Nugent," said Lady Maud, softly, " Gertrude and her parents are the best judges of that part of the question. I will relieve your mind so far as to say that the difficulties in the way of your union with Gertrude are of quite another character."

"Let me hear them, Lady Maud—let me hear them! I know, I trust, how to submit to disappointment even in a matter so very—very near my heart."

Lady Maud, lowering her voice almost to a whisper, replied—

"Mr. Nugent, we have suffered losses from this unfortunate railway. I hardly know to what extent yet; but, although I hope for the best, they **may** be serious."

A flash of satisfaction crossed Nugent's face. He pressed Lady Maud's hand with a cordiality that was rather painful to those slender fingers covered with rings, and exclaimed—

" Is that all ?—is that really all ? Why, Lady Maud, what has money to do with my affection—with my love for Miss Usherwood ? Is not my income, in one way or another, more than twelve hundred a year? And is not that enough for Gertrude and myself—any, and for all of us to live upon ? "

Lady Maud murmured a few more words, and then glided swiftly out of the room in search of her daughter.

Gertrude, notwithstanding all the harrowing anxieties of the day, had not forgotten her toother's words relative to her attachment to Nugent. She could still recall the tone of pity in which her mother uttered the words, " Poor child!" as if she did not indeed withhold her pity and sympathy, but regarded the idea of their union as simply impossible. So she had retired to the drawing-room on Nugent's entrance and was trying to read, but the letter-print danced before her moistened eyes, as we may have seen animalculæ whirling in a drop of water through the glass of a microscope. Next moment she felt, but scarcely saw, her mother by her side. Lady Maud passed her soft arm round her child's neck, and kissing her lips and her eyes, said—

"Dearest, do not tremble so! All is well. Be happy." Then, taking her daughter's arm in hers, she led her back to the hall, and, drawing her towards Nugent, placed her hand in his, and with a winning smile said—

"Take her, Mr. Nugent, and love her dearly, for she deserves it."

And hastening from the room left them together, and returned to her husband's apartment. On the landing she paused for a second, clasped her hands together, and seemed to be silently asking herself some question, for which she found it difficult to find a satisfactory reply. But it was but for a second, and Lady Maud passed upstairs with perfect serenity of manner.

The Codes Of Hammurabi And Moses
W. W. Davies

QTY

The discovery of the Hammurabi Code is one of the greatest achievements of archaeology, and is of paramount interest, not only to the student of the Bible, but also to all those interested in ancient history...

Religion   **ISBN:** *1-59462-338-4*   **Pages:132**
MSRP $12.95

The Theory of Moral Sentiments
Adam Smith

QTY

This work from 1749. contains original theories of conscience amd moral judgment and it is the foundation for systemof morals.

Philosophy **ISBN:** *1-59462-777-0*   **Pages:536**
MSRP $19.95

Jessica's First Prayer
Hesba Stretton

QTY

In a screened and secluded corner of one of the many railway-bridges which span the streets of London there could be seen a few years ago, from five o'clock every morning until half past eight, a tidily set-out coffee-stall, consisting of a trestle and board, upon which stood two large tin cans, with a small fire of charcoal burning under each so as to keep the coffee boiling during the early hours of the morning when the work-people were thronging into the city on their way to their daily toil...

Childrens   **ISBN:** *1-59462-373-2*   **Pages:84**
MSRP $9.95

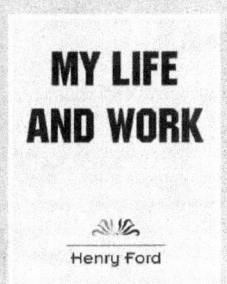

My Life and Work
Henry Ford

QTY

Henry Ford revolutionized the world with his implementation of mass production for the Model T automobile. Gain valuable business insight into his life and work with his own auto-biography... "We have only started on our development of our country we have not as yet, with all our talk of wonderful progress, done more than scratch the surface. The progress has been wonderful enough but..."

Biographies/   **ISBN:** *1-59462-198-5*   **Pages:300**
MSRP $21.95

The Art of Cross-Examination
Francis Wellman

QTY

I presume it is the experience of every author, after his first book is published upon an important subject, to be almost overwhelmed with a wealth of ideas and illustrations which could readily have been included in his book, and which to his own mind, at least, seem to make a second edition inevitable. Such certainly was the case with me; and when the first edition had reached its sixth impression in five months, I rejoiced to learn that it seemed to my publishers that the book had met with a sufficiently favorable reception to justify a second and considerably enlarged edition. ...

Pages:412

Reference   **ISBN: *1-59462-647-2***   *MSRP $19.95*

On the Duty of Civil Disobedience
Henry David Thoreau

QTY

Thoreau wrote his famous essay, On the Duty of Civil Disobedience, as a protest against an unjust but popular war and the immoral but popular institution of slave-owning. He did more than write—he declined to pay his taxes, and was hauled off to gaol in consequence. Who can say how much this refusal of his hastened the end of the war and of slavery ?

Law   **ISBN: *1-59462-747-9***   **Pages:48**

MSRP $7.45

Dream Psychology Psychoanalysis for Beginners
Sigmund Freud

QTY

Sigmund Freud, born Sigismund Schlomo Freud (May 6, 1856 - September 23, 1939), was a Jewish-Austrian neurologist and psychiatrist who co-founded the psychoanalytic school of psychology. Freud is best known for his theories of the unconscious mind, especially involving the mechanism of repression; his redefinition of sexual desire as mobile and directed towards a wide variety of objects; and his therapeutic techniques, especially his understanding of transference in the therapeutic relationship and the presumed value of dreams as sources of insight into unconscious desires.

Pages:196

Psychology   **ISBN: *1-59462-905-6***   *MSRP $15.45*

The Miracle of Right Thought
Orison Swett Marden

QTY

Believe with all of your heart that you will do what you were made to do. When the mind has once formed the habit of holding cheerful, happy, prosperous pictures, it will not be easy to form the opposite habit. It does not matter how improbable or how far away this realization may see, or how dark the prospects may be, if we visualize them as best we can, as vividly as possible, hold tenaciously to them and vigorously struggle to attain them, they will gradually become actualized, realized in the life. But a desire, a longing without endeavor, a yearning abandoned or held indifferently will vanish without realization.

Pages:360

Self Help   **ISBN: *1-59462-644-8***   *MSRP $25.45*

www.**bookjungle**.com *email: sales@bookjungle.com fax: 630-214-0564 mail: Book Jungle PO Box 2226 Champaign, IL 61825*

QTY

☐ **The Rosicrucian Cosmo-Conception Mystic Christianity** *by Max Heindel*   ISBN: *1-59462-188-8*   **$38.95**
The Rosicrucian Cosmo-conception is not dogmatic, neither does it appeal to any other authority than the reason of the student. It is: not controversial, but is: sent forth in the, hope that it may help to clear...   New Age/Religion Pages 646

☐ **Abandonment To Divine Providence** *by Jean-Pierre de Caussade*   ISBN: *1-59462-228-0*   **$25.95**
"The Rev. Jean Pierre de Caussade was one of the most remarkable spiritual writers of the Society of Jesus in France in the 18th Century. His death took place at Toulouse in 1751. His works have gone through many editions and have been republished...   Inspirational/Religion Pages 400

☐ **Mental Chemistry** *by Charles Haanel*   ISBN: *1-59462-192-6*   **$23.95**
Mental Chemistry allows the change of material conditions by combining and appropriately utilizing the power of the mind. Much like applied chemistry creates something new and unique out of careful combinations of chemicals the mastery of mental chemistry...   New Age Pages 354

☐ **The Letters of Robert Browning and Elizabeth Barret Barrett 1845-1846 vol II**   ISBN: *1-59462-193-4*   **$35.95**
by Robert Browning and Elizabeth Barrett   Biographies Pages 596

☐ **Gleanings In Genesis (volume I)** *by Arthur W. Pink*   ISBN: *1-59462-130-6*   **$27.45**
Appropriately has Genesis been termed "the seed plot of the Bible" for in it we have, in germ form, almost all of the great doctrines which are afterwards fully developed in the books of Scripture which follow...   Religion/Inspirational Pages 420

☐ **The Master Key** *by L. W. de Laurence*   ISBN: *1-59462-001-6*   **$30.95**
In no branch of human knowledge has there been a more lively increase of the spirit of research during the past few years than in the study of Psychology, Concentration and Mental Discipline. The requests for authentic lessons in Thought Control, Mental Discipline and...   New Age/Business Pages 422

☐ **The Lesser Key Of Solomon Goetia** *by L. W. de Laurence*   ISBN: *1-59462-092-X*   **$9.95**
This translation of the first book of the "Lernegton" which is now for the first time made accessible to students of Talismanic Magic was done, after careful collation and edition, from numerous Ancient Manuscripts in Hebrew, Latin, and French...   New Age/Occult Pages 92

☐ **Rubaiyat Of Omar Khayyam** *by Edward Fitzgerald*   ISBN:*1-59462-332-5*   **$13.95**
Edward Fitzgerald, whom the world has already learned, in spite of his own efforts to remain within the shadow of anonymity, to look upon as one of the rarest poets of the century, was born at Bredfield, in Suffolk, on the 31st of March, 1809. He was the third son of John Purcell...   Music Pages 172

☐ **Ancient Law** *by Henry Maine*   ISBN: *1-59462-128-4*   **$29.95**
The chief object of the following pages is to indicate some of the earliest ideas of mankind, as they are reflected in Ancient Law, and to point out the relation of those ideas to modern thought.   Religion/History Pages 452

☐ **Far-Away Stories** *by William J. Locke*   ISBN: *1-59462-129-2*   **$19.45**
"Good wine needs no bush, but a collection of mixed vintages does. And this book is just such a collection. Some of the stories I do not want to remain buried for ever in the museum files of dead magazine-numbers an author's not unpardonable vanity..."   Fiction Pages 272

☐ **Life of David Crockett** *by David Crockett*   ISBN: *1-59462-250-7*   **$27.45**
"Colonel David Crockett was one of the most remarkable men of the times in which he lived. Born in humble life, but gifted with a strong will, an indomitable courage, and unremitting perseverance...   Biographies/New Age Pages 424

☐ **Lip-Reading** *by Edward Nitchie*   ISBN: *1-59462-206-X*   **$25.95**
Edward B. Nitchie, founder of the New York School for the Hard of Hearing, now the Nitchie School of Lip-Reading, Inc, wrote "LIP-READING Principles and Practice". The development and perfecting of this meritorious work on lip-reading was an undertaking...   How-to Pages 400

☐ **A Handbook of Suggestive Therapeutics, Applied Hypnotism, Psychic Science**   ISBN: *1-59462-214-0*   **$24.95**
by Henry Munro   Health/New Age/Health/Self-help Pages 376

☐ **A Doll's House: and Two Other Plays** *by Henrik Ibsen*   ISBN: *1-59462-112-8*   **$19.95**
Henrik Ibsen created this classic when in revolutionary 1848 Rome. Introducing some striking concepts in playwriting for the realist genre, this play has been studied the world over.   Fiction/Classics/Plays 308

☐ **The Light of Asia** *by sir Edwin Arnold*   ISBN: *1-59462-204-3*   **$13.95**
In this poetic masterpiece, Edwin Arnold describes the life and teachings of Buddha. The man who was to become known as Buddha to the world was born as Prince Gautama of India but he rejected the worldly riches and abandoned the reigns of power when...   Religion/History/Biographies Pages 170

☐ **The Complete Works of Guy de Maupassant** *by Guy de Maupassant*   ISBN: *1-59462-157-8*   **$16.95**
"For days and days, nights and nights, I had dreamed of that first kiss which was to consecrate our engagement, and I knew not on what spot I should put my lips..."   Fiction/Classics Pages 240

☐ **The Art of Cross-Examination** *by Francis L. Wellman*   ISBN: *1-59462-309-0*   **$26.95**
Written by a renowned trial lawyer, Wellman imparts his experience and uses case studies to explain how to use psychology to extract desired information through questioning.   How-to/Science/Reference Pages 408

☐ **Answered or Unanswered?** *by Louisa Vaughan*   ISBN: *1-59462-248-5*   **$10.95**
Miracles of Faith in China   Religion Pages 112

☐ **The Edinburgh Lectures on Mental Science (1909)** *by Thomas*   ISBN: *1-59462-008-3*   **$11.95**
This book contains the substance of a course of lectures recently given by the writer in the Queen Street Hail, Edinburgh. Its purpose is to indicate the Natural Principles governing the relation between Mental Action and Material Conditions...   New Age/Psychology Pages 148

☐ **Ayesha** *by H. Rider Haggard*   ISBN: *1-59462-301-5*   **$24.95**
Verily and indeed it is the unexpected that happens! Probably if there was one person upon the earth from whom the Editor of this, and of a certain previous history, did not expect to hear again...   Classics Pages 380

☐ **Ayala's Angel** *by Anthony Trollope*   ISBN: *1-59462-352-X*   **$29.95**
The two girls were both pretty, but Lucy who was twenty-one who supposed to be simple and comparatively unattractive, whereas Ayala was credited, as her Bombwhat romantic name might show, with poetic charm and a taste for romance. Ayala when her father died was nineteen...   Fiction Pages 484

☐ **The American Commonwealth** *by James Bryce*   ISBN: *1-59462-286-8*   **$34.45**
An interpretation of American democratic political theory. It examines political mechanics and society from the perspective of Scotsman James Bryce   Politics Pages 572

☐ **Stories of the Pilgrims** *by Margaret P. Pumphrey*   ISBN: *1-59462-116-0*   **$17.95**
This book explores pilgrims religious oppression in England as well as their escape to Holland and eventual crossing to America on the Mayflower, and their early days in New England...   History Pages 268

QTY

The Fasting Cure *by Sinclair Upton*   ISBN: *1-59462-222-1*   **$13.95**
In the Cosmopolitan Magazine for May, 1910, and in the Contemporary Review (London) for April, 1910, I published an article dealing with my experi-
ences in fasting. I have written a great many magazine articles, but never one which attracted so much attention...   New Age/Self Help/Health Pages 164

Hebrew Astrology *by Sepharial*   ISBN: *1-59462-308-2*   **$13.45**
In these days of advanced thinking it is a matter of common observation that we have left many of the old landmarks behind and that we are now pressing
forward to greater heights and to a wider horizon than that which represented the mind-content of our progenitors...   Astrology Pages 144

Thought Vibration or The Law of Attraction in the Thought World   ISBN: *1-59462-127-6*   **$12.95**
by William Walker Atkinson   *Psychology/Religion Pages 144*

Optimism *by Helen Keller*   ISBN: *1-59462-108-X*   **$15.95**
Helen Keller was blind, deaf, and mute since 19 months old, yet famously learned how to overcome these handicaps, communicate with the world, and
spread her lectures promoting optimism. An inspiring read for everyone...   Biographies/Inspirational Pages 84

Sara Crewe *by Frances Burnett*   ISBN: *1-59462-360-0*   **$9.45**
In the first place, Miss Minchin lived in London. Her home was a large, dull, tall one, in a large, dull square, where all the houses were alike, and all the
sparrows were alike, and where all the door-knockers made the same heavy sound...   Childrens/Classic Pages 88

The Autobiography of Benjamin Franklin *by Benjamin Franklin*   ISBN: *1-59462-135-7*   **$24.95**
The Autobiography of Benjamin Franklin has probably been more extensively read than any other American historical work, and no other book of its kind
has had such ups and downs of fortune. Franklin lived for many years in England, where he was agent...   Biographies/History Pages 332

Name	
Email	
Telephone	
Address	
City, State ZIP	

☐ **Credit Card**   ☐ **Check / Money Order**

Credit Card Number	
Expiration Date	
Signature	

Please Mail to: Book Jungle
PO Box 2226
Champaign, IL 61825
or Fax to: 630-214-0564

ORDERING INFORMATION

web: *www.bookjungle.com*
email: *sales@bookjungle.com*
fax: *630-214-0564*
mail: *Book Jungle PO Box 2226 Champaign, IL 61825*
or PayPal *to sales@bookjungle.com*

Please contact us for bulk discounts

DIRECT-ORDER TERMS

20% Discount if You Order
Two or More Books
Free Domestic Shipping!
Accepted: Master Card, Visa,
Discover, American Express